FLEDGLING
Jason Steed

MARK A. COOPER

sourcebooks
jabberwocky

Published by Sourcebooks Jabberwocky, an imprint of Sourcebooks, Inc.
P.O. Box 4410, Naperville, Illinois 60567-4410
(630) 961-3900
Fax: (630) 961-2168
www.jabberwockykids.com

Library of Congress Cataloging-in-Publication data is on file with the publisher.

Source of Production: Versa Press, East Peoria, Illinois, USA
Date of Production: August 2010
Run Number: 13163

Printed and bound in the United States of America.
VP 10 9 8 7 6 5 4 3 2 1

I wish to dedicate this to two very special people:

To Sandra,
who without any doubt is my best friend.

Also dedicated in memory of Raymond V. Steed.
Two months after his fourteenth birthday he joined the ship
Empire Morn as a steward. He died April 26, 1943, at age four-
teen years and 207 days, after an explosion from a German mine
destroyed his ship. He is the youngest recorded service death of
World War II.
Whereas Jason Steed is purely a fictional character, Raymond V.
Steed was a real hero and as such should not be forgotten.
—Mark A. Cooper

Prologue

August 1974

JASON RELEASED THE BRAKE. The plane lurched forward and started to gather speed. He increased the throttle and increased speed. Lights from a vehicle came on ahead. The sirens went off, and the guards poured out of the barracks. Jason slowly pulled back on the tiller. Nothing happened. The plane just continued down the runway.

It bounced and rattled its way toward the buildings. He gave it more power. Still nothing happened when he tried to lift the wheels off the ground for takeoff. The buildings were now getting close; the plane felt lighter to control but would not clear the buildings. He cut the power and applied the brakes.

The plane slowed and bounced to a stop. They were now desperately close to the barracks and Weing's armed guards. Again, he opened the throttles and slowly turned around. He applied the brakes and opened the throttles again. The back of the plane started taking shots from behind.

"Jason. *Go! Go!*" Wilson shouted as he turned the rear machine guns on the oncoming guards. Both Ryan and Peter in their Plexiglas domes turned to the rear and also began shooting.

The tail began receiving heavy fire. The armored jeeps were getting closer and closer. The second jeep had a mounted machine gun and started firing at the plane. Wilson targeted this vehicle and unloaded his rounds. The driver and gunman were killed instantly; the jeep veered off to the left and turned over, bursting into flames.

Wilson was screaming at the top of his lungs for Jason to move, but the noise of the engines drowned any sound he made. Jason pulled the throttles back farther. The plane's old body shook violently.

"This baby is going to need everything to get it off the ground," he said to himself.

He applied more throttle, building up the revs before he eventually released the brakes.

The plane launched forward. He pulled the throttle back farther and farther. With its 110-foot wingspan bouncing, the B-24 stormed down the runway. Now that it was going faster, it felt lighter to control. Jason opened the throttles all the way; he wanted to get as much speed as possible. He pulled back the tiller. The end of the runway and the wire fence rushed toward him. He had to go now. He was going too fast to stop.

The thirty-three-ton plane slowly lifted off the ground and roared into the cloudless dawn sky. Wilson, John, Ryan, and Pete started cheering as they left the complex behind.

Jason turned on the radio to call for help.

"This is Jason Steed of the 22nd Platoon Sea Cadets requesting flight information—over."

═

Ray Steed was on the bridge, He could not believe his ears when the sweet, unbroken voice of his son came loud and clear over the airways. The bridge crew members cheered and gave Ray a pat on the back. Ray had to fight back his emotions.

"This is Jason Steed of the 22nd Platoon Sea Cadets requesting flight information—over," he repeated.

"G'day. Jason Steed, this is Broom Air Force Base North Western Australia. Roger Bankman speaking. Please give your position—over."

"I have no idea, sir. Somewhere over Jakarta, flying southwest, 22 degrees—over."

"We have you on radar. What are you flying, Jason?" Roger replied.

"I don't know, sir. A big American World War II bomber. It has four engines, three domes. It's green, noisy, and bloody huge, sir."

The officers on the bridge of the *Ark Royal*, including Ray, fell about laughing. Then, a new voice came over the airways.

"This is Commander Elliot from Special Forces. Jason Steed, we got your message."

"What message, sir?"

"Are you still in a position to trade for some carrot cake?"

"Wow! You got that? Yes, sir, I want to trade."

"Then, Jason, keep heading toward Broom Airfield. Someone will meet you there."

Eleven years earlier...

Chapter One

March 27, 1963

"THAT'S MY GRANDSON AT the end," said Mr. Macintosh, peering through the window of the maternity ward, making a smudge on the clean glass with his greasy forehead.

"How do you know that's him?" asked Mrs. Macintosh.

"The other two bairns have got teddy bears from their parents. It must be him. The poor wee mite has had no visitors," he replied.

"And you are?" came a very stern voice from behind them. They turned to see a little gray-haired old lady with thin spectacles on her nose, wearing a white nurse's uniform. It was the hospital-appointed nanny, Angela Watson.

"I'm Raymond Steed. I've come to see the baby. These are Mr. and Mrs. Macintosh, my wife's parents."

She shook Mr. Macintosh's hand and said, "It's nice to meet you both. I'm sorry for your loss. I'm Angela Watson." She then turned, put her hands on her hips, and glared at Ray. "I've been looking after Blue. Oh, I called him that because his father has failed to show up for three days and give the poor child a name."

Ray took a breath, chastised. His six-foot-two-inch muscled frame was no match for the tiny gray-haired lady.

She beckoned them into the ward and gently picked up the tiny infant and then passed him to Ray. The baby had faint blond hair already showing on his hairline, and his blue eyes looked around the room. His delicate lips opened and revealed a tiny toothless mouth.

"Oh, my God, he's beautiful. Look at his eyes. Just like our Karen's eyes," Mrs. Macintosh said, trying to fight back the tears and kissing the baby's tiny, soft face.

Tears trickled from Ray's own eyes and down his cheeks as he recalled the events that brought his son into the world.

=

Ray had just returned from his morning run. He took a shower and emerged from a cloud of steam to find Karen sitting on the toilet, looking worried.

"Get dressed, Ray. My water's broken." Without a word, Ray ran into the bedroom and squeezed clothes onto his wet body.

Karen was taken by wheelchair to the delivery room, where Ray was forced to wait outside. He paced up and down the bright-white corridor, waiting for news. Hours had passed when a nurse left the room and ran down the corridor.

"Is everything all right?" he called after her.

Ray got no reply. He now started to worry. He found himself slightly light-headed, so he sat on the cold floor outside the delivery room.

Karen had been so excited. He remembered her beautiful beaming face when she told him the news—the same night he had proposed to her just nine short months ago. He had met Karen on the flight from London to Hong Kong. Ray had just buried his parents and was on his way back to the HMS *Tamar*, the Royal Navy's land base in the British colony Hong Kong, where he was stationed.

When Ray finally heard the wail of a newborn, he jumped to

his feet in excitement. He waited and waited, and still, no one told him anything.

Ray was now starting to panic. He made up his mind that he was going in. As he put his hand to the door, it opened, and a doctor came out.

"Can I go in now, doctor? How is Karen?"

"I am Dr. Collins. I attended your wife's delivery, sir, and what I have to say will be very hard for you."

"What's wrong with the baby?" Ray demanded, preparing himself for the worst.

"The baby? No, sir, the baby is fine. You have a healthy baby boy. It's Mrs. Steed. She had severe internal bleeding that caused a massive heart attack, sir. We could not use a defibrillator to restart her heart until we got the baby safely out. I'm sorry, but she never recovered."

"Why did you save the baby? You should have saved Karen first—damn it. Go back and do something!"

===

As he looked into his son's eyes for the first time, Ray saw that Mrs. Macintosh was right.

"He does have Karen's eyes." He sniffled. "Karen said if we had a boy, he would be named after her father. As part of her wishes, we must call him Jason—Jason Steed."

When you heard the delicate gurgling and saw his head wobbling around and eyes searching the room, you could never have guessed that before he would turn twelve, this tiny bundle would play a major role in the prevention of a nuclear war, but then again, you could never have guessed the kind of boy Jason Steed was…or what was about to make it all begin.

Chapter Two

March 31, 1968

A FEW DAYS AFTER JASON's fifth birthday, he was shopping in Hong Kong with his nanny, Miss Watson. They passed Wong Tong's Karate School. Jason stopped and peered in through the window. Inside, older boys were participating in a martial arts lesson. Jason was fascinated by the moves the boys made. They wore white robes with colored belts and looked to be enjoying what they were doing.

Wong Tong was a tiny Chinese man with a bald head and a long, thin moustache that hung down to his chest. He wore traditional, gold-colored, silk Chinese clothing.

"Jason, come on. We have to get you some new shoes. Your father's coming home from Vietnam tonight. You want to look smart if he takes you out, don't you?"

"What are they doing, Nanny?" Jason asked, pointing his tiny finger at the boys inside.

"That's karate. You're too young for that. You have to wait until you're a big boy like them. That means eating all your vegetables and not just carrot cake," Miss Watson said, pulling his hand and walking off. Jason pulled away and went back to the window, although as soon as he had, he knew he would be in trouble.

He watched her out of the corner of his eye. It was very unusual for him to disobey Miss Watson.

"Jason Steed, you get here right now," she said, looking down at him over the top of her glasses and giving him the "kill look."

"No, I want to do karate," Jason argued. Miss Watson was very surprised by his outburst. She bent down to smack the back of his legs. Jason lifted his leg out of the way, and her hand smacked against the window with a loud bang.

"I want to do karate," Jason repeated.

"You just get here, young man. I don't want to hear another—" By now, Miss Watson's patience had run out. She swiped at his cheek with the back of her hand. This time, Jason dodged her hand to avoid the smack. Jason's head hit the glass window, causing a loud smash, shattering the glass and cutting his forehead open.

Miss Watson immediately pulled out the shards of glass from his cut and placed her hand over the wound to prevent further bleeding. She looked him over to see if he was cut anywhere else.

"An ambulance is coming," a voice called out from the karate dojo. "Can I help?" asked the owner Wong Tong from inside. His English was broken but understandable.

"Thank you for calling the ambulance. Can we come in and get out of the glass? I am so sorry about your window. He is normally a good boy," Miss Watson replied.

"I see whole thing when you bang hand on my window. Why you not let boy do karate? He move very fast to get away from hand that smacks—that is good thing, yes?" Wong Tong asked.

"You call this a good thing?" Miss Watson said, peering at him over her glasses.

"No, boy need teach how to control move."

Jason said nothing. He didn't cry, although he wanted to. While they waited for an ambulance, Jason asked Wong many questions, much to the annoyance of Miss Watson.

The ambulance took them to the local hospital, where Jason received nine stitches. He and Miss Watson returned home to an open front door. The home had been broken into. Thieves had taken the black-and-white television set, a radio, and a small pot of cash Miss Watson kept on the kitchen counter. They had also ransacked the apartment. Clothes, books, and Jason's toys were thrown across the apartment floor. By the time Miss Watson had gotten off the phone with the police, Ray was getting out of a taxi with another man in uniform.

"Dad's here," Jason shouted, looking out the window.

Tired, Ray had returned with a fellow lieutenant, William Giles. Ray had volunteered for duty in Vietnam the same day Jason was released from the hospital. After that, he'd only see his son for short visits every six months or so.

"What on Earth has been going on here?" he shouted.

"Well, I think that's obvious, isn't it? I have called the police. I think I forgot to lock the front door," Miss Watson told Ray.

"You didn't lock the door? Where were you?"

"At the hospital with your disobedient son. Oh, and you also have a glass window to pay for."

"What happened to his head?" Ray demanded angrily.

She went on to explain the events. Partway through, Ray shouted at Jason to go to his room and go to bed. Miss Watson set her jaw. She very carefully told him to calm down and not to raise his voice at her.

Ray paused. He'd just come back from five months in a war

zone. It was only going to be a quick stopover before he would be gone again. Coming back to this and being told by his employee to calm down in front of a fellow officer made the situation worse. One thing led to another, and he accused her of being incapable of looking after a child and a home.

To his surprise, she packed her bags and walked out.

After she left, William and Ray picked up the items around the apartment and dealt with the police. Jason got out of bed and looked through the crack of his bedroom door. In spite of the dressing down, he had hoped his father would come and see him. Once the police left, Ray apologized to William.

"I am sorry you had to come and see this. You can see why I hate coming home."

"I hope you don't mind me saying, Ray, but you don't seem to be very close to your kid. Do you really hate coming home?" William asked.

Ray fell heavily into the couch and sighed. He pulled out a metal toy tank from under the cushion. "Coming back here... reminds me of Karen. The hospital let Karen die, saving the kid. That decision ruined my life." Ray passed William a picture of him and Karen at their wedding. "Now look at the mess I have to come back to."

Jason forced his hand in his mouth to stop the sound of his gasping. The only person he knew well and loved, Miss Watson, had just left—and now this. It was his fault his mother had died? He crept back into bed and cried himself to sleep.

=

Jason awoke the next morning at six to the sound of the front door slamming. Ray had gone out for a run. While his father was out, he got himself dressed and had a breakfast of milk and carrot cake. William was still sleeping on the couch. Jason was attempting to wash his glass clean when his father came back. He did not want to be too much trouble. He had even attempted to make his own bed.

"Morning, Jason. How is your head?" asked Ray.

"Okay, thank you, sir," came the quiet reply. Jason never looked his father in the eye.

Ray said nothing.

"Hey, kid, can you get me a glass of milk?" William asked Jason.

"Yes, sir." Jason poured a glass of milk for William

Ray sat on the couch beside his friend. "So, tell me, Jason, how is school? Have you many friends? And please tell me how you managed to 'head butt' a window at a karate studio."

"It's called a dojo, not a studio. School is okay. I have a few friends. Can I go now, sir?" Jason replied, passing a glass of milk to William and still refusing to look at his father.

"Go where? You haven't seen me for nearly six months. No, you can't go. I have to take a shower. Then, we have to go to the karate studio—sorry, dojo—and pay for the damages you caused. After that, find a new nanny and buy a TV."

Jason sat back down at the kitchen table and gazed out the window at the other apartments. He still did not know his father's friend's name. He was unhappy that the man was staying in his home and taking his father's attention, but he had to make the best of it. "I am Jason Steed, sir," he announced as he walked over and held out his hand to introduce himself. "This is my house."

"Pleased to meet you, Jason. Because your dad never introduced us, I'm William Giles. You may call me Bill." He smiled, shaking Jason's hand.

Ray stood and walked toward Jason's bedroom and beckoned to his son. His dad sat on the bed.

"Close the door behind you."

Jason followed with his head bowed. He looked up at his father through his blond hair that just covered his eyes.

"You and I need to sort something out. Don't you ever talk to an adult like that again. Do you hear me?" Ray whispered.

"But I did not know who he was."

"That is not the point. You could just ask. Now, I want you to promise me you will start to behave."

"Yes, sir," Jason replied, still looking through his hair.

"Stop calling me 'sir.' It's Dad. Also, we need to get your hair cut. I can't see your eyes. It's much too long in the front. Make sure you're ready to go in five minutes. Officer Giles won't be joining us."

"Yes, Dad."

———

When they arrived at the karate dojo, Ray paused outside. It was boarded up with a large piece of plywood painted with the words "Open as usual." Ray walked in without checking to see if Jason had kept up. Jason followed, red faced and out of breath.

"Hello. Is anyone here?" Ray called out to the empty room. Wong Tong walked out from behind a black screen and bowed. Jason in turn bowed. Ray looked at him and shook his head in annoyance.

"Hello, sir. You are boy's father?" Wong Tong asked.

"Yes, sir. I'm very sorry about your window. I am here to pay for it. Jason's here to apologize. How much do I owe you, sir?" Ray asked.

"Twenty dollars, sir. That will take care of damage."

Ray pulled out his wallet and took out the cash to pay Wong Tong. "Jason, have you something to say?"

"Sorry, Mr. Wong Tong." A smile crept across his face. "Can I come to your karate dojo and learn karate?"

"Out of the question, Jason. That is not what you were supposed to say," his father snapped back.

"But, Dad, please."

"Are you answering me back?" Ray hissed, his eyes like ice. Jason froze and said no more.

"Why you not let boy do karate? He can move very fast. I teach good and teach discipline," Wong Tong said with his arms folded.

Without a word, Ray grabbed Jason by the arm and hurried out of the dojo. He marched Jason to a large building and told him to wait outside. For what seemed like nearly an hour, Jason watched the traffic drive up and down the busy Hong Kong street. Finally, Ray appeared from the building, carrying some papers.

"Okay, your new nanny comes tomorrow. She is Chinese and has great references. Now let's go and get your hair cut."

The barbershop was filled with smoke. It had three chairs for cutting hair and a long wooden bench to sit on and wait. The barbers were all Chinese and spoke broken English. They all worked fast.

Jason hated the front of his haircut. He did not mind the back and sides, but he preferred the front long to cover his eyes. He thought no one could see him, and it made him feel secure.

"Boy, you sit here," the barber told Jason as he put a small plank of wood across the chair's arms. Jason slowly sat down and looked at himself in the mirror. He could see his father looking at him from behind. He tried to think of a way to avoid the front of his hair being cut as the barber trimmed the back and sides military short. As he was about to cut the front, Jason yelled out, "Ouch, that hurts! It's pulling my stitches."

"I not touch stitches," said the startled barber. Jason jumped down, holding his head.

"It's okay, Jason. Don't be a baby. He will not hurt your stitches. Get back up in the chair," his father said, trying to reassure him.

"The doctor said I must not touch the stitches. He will pull them out, and he hurt me," Jason protested. He knew he was pushing his luck. It was obvious that the barber had not touched Jason's forehead.

Ray was embarrassed. People in the barbershop were now looking at him. "How much do I owe you?" he asked the barber.

Once outside, Ray grabbed Jason by the arm and dragged him down an alley. Jason wanted to protest, but he thought he should keep quiet. The space was thin and dark and smelled unpleasant like rotting vegetables. Ray grabbed Jason and pulled him over his knee. He then whacked his son's backside six times. Jason's eyes filled with tears, and his lower lip quivered; however, he remained silent.

"I told you to behave. You and I both know he never got

anywhere near your stitches. This is what you will get if you want to start acting up. Do you want more?"

Jason shook his head in silence. There was no arguing with his father. He knew that now.

═

When they arrived home, Jason went to his room and gazed out the window. From here, he could see the Royal Marines assault course. He spent many hours watching the marines and navy personnel climbing the ropes and obstacles while being shouted at by a drill instructor.

William had left already, and that was fine by Ray. He was feeling guilty for being so estranged from his own son but could not see a way of getting close to him. He thought about sending Jason to live with his grandparents in Scotland. All he seemed to be doing was shouting or spanking. Was he raised in fear? No, he wasn't.

═

The following morning, Ray answered a knock on the door to find the new nanny: a young, athletic Chinese lady.

"You must be Mai Lee?" Ray asked, holding out his hand as he invited her in. They spent a few minutes talking, and Ray called to his son.

Jason skulked out of his room, an unhappy look on his face. The idea of a new nanny was not pleasant for a five-year-old. He had grown to love Miss Watson.

"Hello. You must be Jason? I am Mai Lee," she said, offering her hand. Jason halfheartedly shook her hand and nodded. The room went quiet.

"Jason, have you lost your tongue?" Ray barked.

"Hello," he said quietly.

She knelt down to make eye contact with him. "You look so sad, Jason. Did you like your previous nanny?" she asked.

Jason nodded.

"Maybe you're just shy?"

"No, he's not shy. He's not afraid to say anything," Ray interrupted.

"I am sure you will grow to like me. Now, Jason, if we are to get on, I need to know what you like and don't like. What is your favorite drink?" she asked.

"Milk," Jason replied.

She gently held both his hands. "Good, milk is good for you. And food—what is your favorite food?"

"Carrot cake."

"Carrot cake? I don't know what this is. Is it a cake made from carrots?" she laughed.

"Yes, and it has cream on the top. They sell it in the store. Miss Watson always buys it," he replied.

She spoke to him more. Then, Jason used his finger to part his hair, revealing his eyes. Ray watched his son closely. It was the first time he had seen his son smile since he had been home. Ray knelt down in front of Jason, watching his son's eyes sparkle like deep-blue sapphire, the same color as Karen's. His white teeth shone through his cheeky but adorable smile. He smiled just like his mother. Jason noticed his father staring at him and stopped talking.

14

"Tell me more, Jason," Mai Lee asked. "What sports do you like to play?"

Jason seized the opportunity. "I am not allowed to play sports," he said, looking down to the floor and putting his sad face back on.

Ray stiffened. "Why? That's nonsense, Jason. Of course you can play sports. I expect it of you. I was good at sports and still am. Your mother competed in the Olympic Games and won a bronze medal. You can do any sport, son. It's in your genes. You should be really good at it." Ray realized he was trying to bring Jason's smile back. He wasn't succeeding.

Jason looked at his father and made direct eye contact.

"Dad, you said I can't have karate lessons."

Ray knew he was now backed into a tight corner. He smiled at his cunning son and nodded. "You can have karate lessons at Wong Tong's."

Clumsily, Jason reached out and hugged his father. Ray quickly stood.

"Mr. Steed, Wong Tong teaches boys from age eight to adult. I don't think he will teach someone who is barely five," Mai Lee said.

"In Jason's case, he will. He has already offered."

Chapter Three

KARATE LESSONS WERE ONCE a week. Wong Tong told Jason that if he worked hard, he could get a black belt in four to five years; however, Jason was far too impatient to wait that long. He studied hard for each category. To pass a new colored belt in karate, you had to show you could memorize certain moves. These moves were called "katas." Jason made sure to learn a new move each week.

After just four weeks, Wong Tong agreed to allow him to take the test for his yellow belt. Jason took it one step further and asked if he could take his orange belt at the same time. Reluctantly, Wong Tong agreed and was surprised to see Jason pass. Jason then asked if he could take his green belt.

"You will fail," Wong told him. After Jason insisted, Wong agreed, thinking Jason would learn a valuable lesson. Wong was wrong. Jason passed his green belt too. Mai Lee had just enough money on her to pay for three exams.

Over the next few weeks, he studied for his blue belt. By the time his father was due to come back for his next visit two months later, Jason was studying for his brown belt. Wong Tong was also giving him additional one-on-one lessons. He had never seen a student so gifted and enthusiastic before.

"You have talents," he told Jason. "But do not allow them to make your head swell."

Ray came back to an empty house. The apartment was very clean. Fresh flowers sat in a vase on the kitchen table. He went to the fridge to look for a drink and laughed to himself when he saw the amount of milk and carrot cake stored there. He looked around the apartment and went into Jason's room. The room was covered with karate posters and pictures of a young actor named Bruce Lee. Above Jason's bed were white, yellow, green, and blue belts.

On his bedside table was a framed picture of Karen collecting her bronze medal at the Olympics. Ray had never seen this picture before. Maybe Karen's parents had sent it to the boy.

The front door slammed opened, and he could hear the sound of running feet. Jason ran into the room, and to Ray's delight and surprise, he threw his arms around his neck naturally and easily. He spoke so fast about his karate that Ray could hardly understand what he was saying. He sat on Jason's bed, pulled his son onto his lap, and watched him talk.

"Jason, I have some news. We have to go home for two weeks. I have an invitation to go to a garden party at Buckingham Palace. Do you know who lives there?" Ray asked.

"Home? This is home, Dad," Jason replied, confused.

"No, son, we have a house in England that my parents left me. That's home. Now, tell me who lives at Buckingham Palace?"

He smiled. "The queen. Can Mai Lee come too, Dad?"

"No, it will just be me and you. We have to leave tonight. I will ask Mai Lee to pack some things for you."

"Can I still go to karate? Can you come and watch? Did you see the belts I've gotten? Watch this move," Jason said.

He then jumped off his father's lap and stood showing his father a high kick.

"If I have time, I will come and watch you. I have a lot to do before we fly."

Jason replied with a thank-you in Cantonese.

Mai Lee was teaching him. When he talked in the home, he was only allowed to speak in Chinese. He also spoke to Wong Tong in Chinese. When he learned of all this, Ray could only think that Mai Lee was taking Jason to karate and teaching him how to speak. Ray never made it back in time to watch his son.

=

When they arrived at London's Heathrow Airport, Ray called his uncle, Stewart Steed, and asked to be collected and driven to the house.

The two men shook hands as they met. Stewart, wearing his monocle, bent down to shake Jason's hand. Jason stared at his gray handlebar moustache and wondered how his uncle Stewart prevented his monocle from falling out.

"Welcome to England, Jason. It's nice to finally meet you at last. Well, what do you think of your country?"

"My country is Hong Kong, sir. Is it always this cold here?" Jason replied.

Stewart laughed out loud.

An hour later, after a drive that had Jason pinned to the window until he started yawning, the Jaguar pulled up outside the estate. Ray jumped out and opened one of the large black iron gates. As they drove up the gravel driveway to the large white house, Stewart asked, "What do you think of your home, Jason?"

No reply came. Jason lay asleep on the backseat.

Ray carried Jason inside and put him in his old bed. He gave Jason a kiss and whispered, "I guess this is going to be your room now, son."

Nine hours passed before Jason awoke. It was cold in the house. He climbed out of bed, still dressed, and looked around the large bedroom. It had a polished wooden floor with a center rug, and some framed certificates, which were too high for him to attempt to read, dressed the walls. The dressing table was full of trophies for football, rugby, and tennis—all had his father's name on them.

The view outside the bedroom window was completely foreign to him. The house was surrounded by a lawn large enough for three football fields. Around the perimeter, large oak trees proudly spread their branches out in all directions. At the front of the lawn was the long and winding gravel driveway that finished at the black iron gates. Outside the locked gates, traffic rushed up and down the main road.

Jason made his way to the door and slowly opened it. There was a stairway on each side of the landing, swooping down to the front hall. He walked down the stairs slowly, his tiny figure dwarfed by the huge house. He heard music from one of the rooms and found his father in the kitchen, reading papers and tapping his foot in time to the Beatles' "Hey Jude."

"Morning, Jason, how are you?" Ray asked.

"Has this house got a toilet?" Jason winced, standing cross-legged.

Ray laughed and got up from his seat. "No, it has four toilets. You passed two upstairs and another just outside—that door on your left."

Jason returned minutes later. "Can I have some milk please, Dad?"

Ray picked up his jacket. "Go and get your shoes. I left them by your bed. We will go out to a café for breakfast. There's no food in the house yet."

Jason ran upstairs and soon came running down with his shoe-laces flapping.

"Do them up. You will break your neck coming down the stairs like that," his father ordered. Jason bent down and tried doing his laces on one shoe. Ray looked down to see what was taking so long. He had almost done it, but when he pulled the two loops, the knot came apart.

"You do know how to do it, don't you?" Eventually, Ray bent down and helped him. *Of course, slippers and sandals only in Hong Kong*, he realized. His son had so much to learn about his true home.

As they opened the front door, a large gust of icy cold wind came in.

"You need to get your coat on, Jason. I put your suitcase at the foot of your bed. Run and get it, and I will start the car."

"I don't have a coat, do I?" Jason asked.

Ray frowned at him. "Why not? I told Mai Lee to buy you clothes when you need them."

"I don't need a coat at home," Jason said and shrugged. Ray took off his jacket and hung it on Jason's shoulders. It almost dragged along the floor it was so long on him.

"I will buy you one later, and you need to get your hair cut again."

The pair set off in what had once been Ray's parents' car, a 1962 Rover 100. It was black with red leather seats. Jason knelt on the backseat so he could see out the windows. His unwashed and uncombed hair stuck up in all directions.

After a short journey, they stopped and ate at a small café. Jason loved the food of Great Britain: eggs, bacon, and beans like he had never tasted before. Later, his father bought him a coat and some new "slip-on" shoes at Harrods.

This was a whole new experience for Ray. He had never before had to buy clothes for his son, help bathe him, or wash his hair. He had always had a nanny to do this for him. And all the while, he marveled at his son. Jason could do most things for himself, and he was still only a five-year-old boy.

Chapter Four

THE FOLLOWING DAY, FATHER and son set off in their best clothes to Buckingham Palace for the garden party. Ray wore his naval uniform. It was customary to invite some officers, and Ray knew he'd been asked for earning the Queen's Award for Bravery a few years earlier when he saved the life of a Scottish fisherman.

On the way to the palace, he instructed Jason on how to behave. "Just be yourself and remember: 'yes, sir' or 'yes, ma'am.' They won't expect anything else from someone your age."

It was at least sunny and not too cold. Once inside, the duke, the queen's husband, walked over to Ray and shook his hand. He was an ex-naval man himself and enjoyed talking to navy personnel. The duke was tall and stood very upright, and he spoke with an upper-class British accent like Uncle Stewart. He told Jason, "My children are playing over there. Please go and join them."

Jason walked off toward the children. They were running around playing "touch."

The queen and the duke had four children: Cuthbert, age fourteen; Louise, twelve; Henry, ten; and Catherine, almost five. Jason looked at the children running around. He was not one for playing games. To him, it looked like a waste of time.

Jason walked off down to the palace gardens, which started at the end of a long, well-manicured lawn. A neatly trimmed hedge surrounded two huge weeping willow trees. In the center of the trees was a large pond with some very expensive koi carp given to the queen from the Japanese prime minister.

Jason walked over to the pond and sat at the edge, watching the fish. The pond was very deep and had a stone lion in the center with water pouring from its mouth.

"Do you like apples?" A tiny voice came from behind the trees. Jason looked up and could just see a small figure through the trees. As he walked through the weeping willow branches, he saw a little girl about his age wearing a pretty white and pink dress. She had curly blond hair with pink bows. She held her dress up, trying to hold as many apples as she could pick up. She did not seem to mind that she was revealing her underwear.

"Yes, I like apples. May I pick one myself?" Jason asked walking under the apple tree. She looked at Jason and smiled. He reached to the lower branches and picked an apple.

"Let me check it. If it has a maggot in it, you will be ill," she said, sitting down on the grass and spilling her apples around her. She took the apple from Jason and studied it. She took a bite.

"It's a good one," she said with a mouthful of apple, passing it back to Jason, who sat down next to her. Jason took a large bite, and they smiled at each other.

"I'm Catherine. I will be five on Wednesday. What is your name?"

"Jason Steed. I was five two months ago."

Jason wasn't sure how much time passed. He only knew that he was having more fun than he'd had since he'd arrived. Catherine showed him how to make daisy chains. She put one around his neck. He made a bracelet for her wrist. They also searched for four-leaf clovers. She told him they would bring him good luck if either he or she could find one.

"Look, a maggot," Catherine said. It wriggled in her fingers. "I am going to feed it to the fish." Jason followed her to the pond. She held the maggot at arm's length and let it dangle, attracting the koi carp.

"Catherine, get away. You can't swim!" a voice shouted.

It was Cuthbert. Startled, she lost her balance and fell into the water with a splash. The onlookers shrieked and started running. Catherine had gone under and had not come back up. Even the queen herself picked up her dress and ran. Jason didn't hesitate. He simply dove in.

The pond was icy cold. It was like being hit by a cricket bat. As he struggled with the weight of the water pulling on his clothes, he kicked off his shoes, wriggled out of his new coat, and reached for Catherine. His hand found her soft, warm arm, and he pulled her up. Once she had her head out of the water and had taken a breath, she started to panic, pushing Jason under the water. He came up and grabbed a breath of air, got under her body, and pushed it toward the edge. She was screaming and choking. He held his breath and continued to push her toward the edge. She was very heavy, but he summoned enough strength to pull her up out of the water.

Catherine shivered on all fours, coughing and crying. Jason put his hand on her back and tried to comfort her.

Ray outpaced the other guests and arrived first. He scooped Catherine up in his arms and started carrying her back toward the palace. Jason, who now had also lost a sock, followed behind, pulling out slimy water weeds from his hair.

The duke took Catherine from Ray. She was coughing and crying. "I believe she may have swallowed some water," Ray informed him.

"What was one doing by the pond, dear?" asked the queen, wiping the girl's face with her hand. They carried her into the palace. Ray turned and looked down at Jason. He still had pond weed on his face and head.

"Sorry, Dad, I lost my new coat, shoes, and a sock." He pointed down to his bare pink foot. For a moment, he feared his father was going to be enraged, but Ray broke into a shaky smile and then laughed as he bent down and picked him up.

"You have no idea how proud of you I am, son. Well done, Jason. Gosh, you are cold. We better get you out of these wet clothes."

———

The following morning, Ray was up early as normal and took a run around the house grounds—a two-mile course. As he approached the house, he heard a strange noise. It sounded like someone crying out in pain. As he rounded the corner, he found Jason barefoot, wearing just his underwear.

He was performing his karate katas.

For a few minutes, Ray stood watching his son perform the movements with precision, speed, and grace. At each strike or kick, Jason gave a "keeah" shout.

Just as Ray got dressed, the doorbell rang. He walked to the front door and saw a man with a black car parked down at the front gates. Ray hurried down to greet him.

The stranger looked to be in his late fifties and was slightly overweight, wearing a black suit and tie. He had balding gray hair and looked very pale too. His appearance reminded Ray of an undertaker.

"Can I help you, sir?" Ray asked.

"I am Archibald, her majesty's head butler. I have an invitation for Master Jason Steed," Archibald said, passing a sealed letter to Ray through the gate.

"Thank you, sir," Ray said, opening the envelope. After he read it, he gave a broad smile.

"Archibald, is it customary to bring a gift? I have no idea what is expected at a kid's party. Any ideas for a five-year-old princess?" Ray asked.

"Sir, I would let Jason choose something. Can I inform the palace he will be attending?" Archibald asked.

"Yes, he will be there. It's an honor. Thank you." Ray walked into the house and found Jason standing at the fridge, drinking milk directly from the glass bottle.

"Is that how a guest of the princess behaves?" Ray asked, startling Jason. He jumped and spilled some milk down his chest.

"What guest of a princess?" Jason asked, puzzled.

Ray wiped off his milk moustache and passed the invitation to Jason.

Jason looked at the note. He could read his name and some of the other words but failed to make any sense of the message. After a few minutes, Ray pointed at the words with Jason and helped him read them:

Master Jason Steed. Her Royal Highness Princess Catherine invites you to her fifth birthday party on Wednesday, 2:00 p.m.

It was signed by Catherine in her own writing.

"Dad, I can't go. Nana and Granddad Macintosh are coming from Scotland to see us before we go home."

"They are coming today. The party is tomorrow. Now, put the milk away or get a glass, and don't drink out of the bottle again. What sort of impression will that give your grandparents?"

"It will show them I do just as my dad does," Jason said, giving a cheeky grin.

===

When the Macintoshes arrived, they started weeping. Jason was confused, but he said nothing. His grandparents had spoken on the phone and seen pictures, but they had not seen him since their daughter's funeral. His grandmother kept kissing him, and Jason found the affection a little overwhelming. He did enjoy hearing stories about his mother when she was a child.

Ray asked if Mrs. Macintosh would give Jason's hair a cut. Jason insisted on leaving his blond hair long enough in front to cover his eyes. Because she did not want to upset her only grandchild, she agreed, leaving his blond bangs down over his eyes. Ray said nothing. He wasn't even terribly annoyed. He had gotten used to seeing his son's hair like this.

===

The following afternoon, Ray took Jason back to Harrods to buy a gift for Catherine. Jason chose a pair of inflatable armbands. He thought her father should teach her to swim. Once they arrived at the palace, Jason was surprised by the attention he got. Some of the palace security and police came and shook his hand. They called him "our little hero."

Jason followed a footman through the great halls of the palace. He looked up at the huge paintings and large sculptures. The hallways were bigger than anything he had ever seen before. He passed door after door until they arrived at a long corridor where Henry, Cuthbert, and Louise were waiting.

"Giles, we will take Jason to the party," Cuthbert told the footman. Jason, still nervous, smiled and nodded. He followed them into a large room. Pink and white balloons hung from the ceiling. The Beatles played in the background. In the center of the room was a large table full of colorful food. He could see Catherine in the corner sitting on the floor with a group of girls around her age.

"Jason Steed, welcome and please let me say thank you. You are our hero. We will never forget what you did," the duke said, shaking Jason's hand. The girls and Catherine looked up when they heard his name and stared at Jason. He started to blush when the queen walked in front of him, holding out her hand.

"Hello, Jason. May I say how grateful we all are? We owe you a great debt for your courage," her majesty said.

"Thank you, ma'am" was the barely audible reply.

Catherine came and thanked him for coming. They sat next to each other at the large table and ate. She promised Jason that she would learn to swim. Jason did not join in the party games; he just wanted to watch. Later, she showed Jason her new dolls, something he hated but went along with.

As the party ended, Catherine wanted to walk with Jason down to meet his father. When they said good-bye, she leaned forward and kissed him. It stunned Jason. He had never been kissed by a girl before, but he liked it.

Once in the car, his father teased him. "Boy oh boy, you are starting early."

===

Back in Hong Kong, it took Jason almost a year to complete his black belt in tae kwon do. Once he had it, he wanted to learn more. Wong Tong had told him once of an ancient form of Japanese martial art called jujitsu. It was an art that used the opponent's strength and force of attack as a weapon against him. In Hong Kong, there was a dojo and a grand master. The other students at Jason's dojo had talked about this mysterious old man who had spent his life training in jujitsu. He would only teach twelve students at any one time and only taught the very best. Jason asked Mai Lee to take him, but she refused, saying it would be a waste of time. Plus, Wong Tong still had much to teach him.

Jason was normally put to bed at seven o'clock each night, but he could never sleep for more than an hour or so at a time. One night, after Mai Lee had put him to bed, he got up, dressed, and climbed out of his window. He crept through his backyard and climbed the eight-foot wire fence into the marine's assault course. For two hours, he climbed the rope ladders, ran the courses, and crawled through the tunnels. Every single night, he would go there and spend as much time training as he could. He used a stopwatch his uncle Stewart had given him as a gift.

When he wasn't at school, he would time the marines around the course. The fastest marine he timed was seven minutes and six seconds. The slowest was nine minutes and eighteen seconds. His own time was over fifteen minutes, but each night, he got faster and faster. Eventually, he could complete the course in less than ten minutes. Mai Lee could never understand how Jason's knees and hands were always dirty, cut, and bruised in the morning.

=

Later that fall, Jason wore Mai Lee down, and she agreed to take him to see the grand master at the jujitsu dojo. Jason wore his karate gi with his black belt. They had to wait two hours before they were shown in.

Jason bowed as he entered. "Grand master, I would like to be a student of jujitsu please," he said.

The grand master looked the small boy up and down and asked, "What is that belt? What school?"

"It's a black belt for tae kwon do, sir."

"You are too small, boy. How old?" came his rapid reply.

"Six, sir."

The grand master nodded and smiled.

"Okay, you come back before you are eight with two more black belts from two different schools, and I'll teach you."

The task was impossible, but Jason respected the grand master enough not to argue. He thanked him, bowed, and left. The same day, Jason enrolled in the judo school held at HMS *Tamar*, and on the following day, he enrolled at a Shotokan dojo. He also continued to go to Wong Tong's dojo twice a week.

The judo was the hardest for him to master. He was only six after all. The next youngest student in the group was ten. This style was a lot more physical. He struggled and grew tired of constantly being thrown on his back, but the lessons he learned about defending himself against bigger and heavier opponents would help him in ways he could not even imagine.

═

By the time he was nearly eight, Jason went to his first competition. He was especially excited because his father was home and had promised to watch.

As it turned out, Ray never showed up.

Jason spent much of the time watching the door to see if his father would come. He was so distracted that he lost in the final round to a thirteen-year-old boy. Wong Tong saw it as a victory, for Jason was half the size of his opponent and could have won—that is, if he had concentrated. The victory was in the lesson.

Jason passed his extra two black belts and also collected a second Dan black belt (a higher grade in tae kwon do). On top of that, Jason was learning to speak Japanese from his karate instructor at the Shotokan dojo. He was ready to talk to the grand master once again.

═

Now eight, bigger, and wearing a smart new gi, Jason walked himself to the jujitsu dojo to apply. The grand master sat in a large gold and red throne-like chair. His students sat cross-legged around him. Jason recognized Jet Chan, a thirteen-year-old karate champion. His picture was often in martial arts magazines. Jason approached, carrying a black belt in each hand and his second Dan black belt around his waist, and then bowed.

"Hello, grand master. Thank you for seeing me again," Jason said in his broken Japanese. "I have two additional black belts, plus a second Dan in tae kwon do, sir. Please, can I become a student, sir?"

The grand master looked very surprised to hear him speaking in his native tongue and nodded. He replied in English.

"When is your eighth birthday, boy?"

"Yesterday, sir."

"I see. So, you failed me. I told you to return before you are eight."

Jason looked stunned. "Yesterday was Sunday, sir. I collected my black belt from judo on Saturday," Jason argued.

"I don't accept excuses. You failed. However, you have done very well for one so small. Come back in six months with another black belt, and I will consider it."

Jason was so angry that he started to shake. He had learned from his first nanny, Miss Watson, how to deliver a look that could kill and planted "the look" on the grand master.

It was impossible to get a new black belt in six months. He felt he had done more than he had been asked to do. He noticed Jet Chan laughing at him. Jason turned and started to walk away. He hoped this movement would show disrespect.

"Boy," Jet Chan called out.

Jason, whose eyes were welling up, stopped and turned.

"You have all these belts and yet you are not honorable. You should know you bow before you leave. If you don't, it is a sign of disrespect," Jet Chan said.

Jason took a few steps forward. "Martial arts is honor, respect, and discipline. How can your grand master teach me honor when he has none?" Jason replied. Again, he turned to walk away.

Jet Chan stood in his path.

"How dare you insult our dojo and the grand master. There is an old Japanese saying—"

"I don't want to hear your old Japanese saying. There is an old British saying—up yours."

A gasp erupted from the students. Jason's pulse picked up a notch. The students formed a circle around him, standing ready to attack. Jason dropped his belts, crouched in a fighting stance, and stood ready on his toes, ready to protect himself despite the odds. What a fool he had been, he told himself. He would be very lucky to get out without any broken bones. For a few tense moments, his attention was on every move and sound around him.

The grand master stood and gave a loud clap of his hands and told his students to stand down. He admired the courage of Jason. He nodded a slight bow to Jason and gestured with his hand for him to go. No one had ever stood up to him before, and perhaps he had been a little hard on the boy. But he didn't change his mind. With a wave of his gnarled hand, Jason was dismissed.

=

By April 1973, Jason had just turned ten—and he had a new black belt in kung fu and a third Dan in tae kwon do.

Wong Tong entered him into a competition. He would have to fight in the under-fifteen-years-old category. Many of his opponents would be up to five years older than him, but Wong Tong said he was more than ready.

Meanwhile, Jason had expanded his nighttime activities. He continued to practice on the assault course, but he had also found a way to break into the flight simulator room. The small window in the men's toilet was never locked, so he could climb up and pull himself in.

At night, he taught himself to fly a variety of aircraft and helicopters. It was like a huge game for him. At first, he would crash, but slowly, he mastered how to take off, fly, and land.

Ray came home to Hong Kong the day before the competition. He told Jason he had some great news to tell him but wanted to wait until after the competition. He never did explain why he'd missed the competition two years before.

Maybe he has a girlfriend, Jason told himself.

===

The night before the competition started like any other. Jason climbed the fence into the military base. He finished the assault course in less than seven minutes and made his way to the flight simulator, unaware he was being watched.

While he was flying a helicopter in the simulator, the door burst open. Frozen in panic, Jason didn't even attempt to struggle as two burly MPs grabbed him and dragged him to a cell in the military police offices. His heart raced. He was terrified of what his father would do when he found out. He was also worried that his father would get into trouble for what he'd done.

"You have been seen sneaking around the base a number of times. We have been getting reports for months now of a young boy running between the buildings. This is a government complex, and it is a high breach of security," one of his captors informed him.

After ten minutes in a cell, they took him into a small interview room. The room was painted a light gray, and it had no windows.

"What is your name?" the sweatier, heavier MP asked.

Jason was worried. He did not wish to get his father into trouble and did not know how to get out of this. As he looked up through his blond fringe of hair, he replied in Chinese.

"I am John Lennon." It was the first name that popped into his head.

"Speak English. What is your name?" the MP demanded and banged his hand on the table.

Jason shook his head, as if he did not understand. One MP left and came back a few minutes later with a female MP who had short hair like a man.

"He is not Chinese. Look at him. What is your name, son?" she demanded.

Jason shook his head.

"What is your name?" she asked in Chinese.

"John Lennon," Jason replied.

"Okay, smart-ass, and I am the queen, and these two officers are Ringo Starr and George Harrison."

Again, Jason refused to answer.

The overweight MP took a photo.

"Take him to a cell," he ordered.

As they locked the door, he said, "Just give us your name, and we'll get your parents and you can go home."

Jason ignored them. He had to keep this from his father… somehow. It was a square room with a small toilet in the corner, a wooden bunk, and a stained mattress. There was a chair with an orange plastic seat and black metal legs too. Jason paced up and down, trying to think. He knew he had to get out by the morning. If not, Mai Lee and his father would report him missing, and the military police would reveal who they had in custody. He pulled at the bars on the window. As he did, he looked at the screws holding them to the wall.

He looked around the room, picked up the chair, and put it back on the floor on one leg. He used all his weight to try and bend the leg, but it wouldn't budge. He had been told in school not to rock back on a similar chair because the legs would bend or break.

"That just shows teachers don't know everything," he hissed to himself in anger. The more he tried, the angrier he became. He stuck the chair leg against the wall and pushed with his feet by using the end of the bunk. He rocked and used all his strength. Eventually, the thin tubular leg bent.

It took thirty minutes before the constant bending back and forth caused the leg to break, leaving a very sharp edge. Jason pulled the bunk under the window. Standing on the bed and using the broken leg, he managed to unscrew the screws on one of the bars.

Once the bar was down, only the glass held him prisoner. Using the chair, he smashed the window. As he was trying to clear the shards, he could hear the keys in the cell door. He took off his sweater and placed it on the bottom of the window and started to climb out. A hand caught his ankle.

"Gotcha," came a voice. He pulled Jason back in, but Jason refused to let go of the remaining bars.

He used his other foot to kick the guard in the face, causing him to let go. Jason started to climb back out the window only to see the fat MP outside waiting to catch him. Jason climbed back into the cell. The guard had blood pouring from his nose. Jason ducked down and ran past him. He slammed the cell door and, using the keys still in the lock, trapped the guard in the cell.

As he sprinted down the corridor, he knew he was in big trouble. Another guard came around the corner. Jason ran at him and launched into a flying kick, catching the guard directly in the chest. The guard grabbed at Jason and managed to grab his arm as they both fell to the floor. Jason grabbed the guard's other hand and bent his fingers back. The guard yelled out in pain and released him.

Furious, the fat MP was now coming in the front door, his nightstick in his hand. Jason ran into the office and picked up a chair and threw it at the window, but to his surprise, the glass didn't break. From the corner of his eye, Jason saw the fat MP raise his nightstick. Jason dropped to the floor on his hands and spun around, sweeping the legs out from under the MP. As the MP fell to the floor, Jason picked the fire extinguisher off the wall and threw it.

This time, the window gave and sent glass flying outside over another two MPs who were racing to assist. Jason jumped through the window and ran as fast as he could. Two MPs chased Jason on foot while one followed in a Land Rover.

Up ahead, Jason could see the head lamps of another MP's Land Rover heading directly toward him. Jason kept sprinting straight at the vehicle. He knew he had to get to the assault course, as they could not drive there. With just a few feet to spare, Jason turned off the road onto the course. Six MPs climbed out of the Land Rovers and chased him on foot.

Jason knew every inch of the course and was used to being here after dark. He had the upper hand. When he disappeared into the shadows with a surge of confidence, he lost them.

Minutes later, he climbed the fence into his yard and retreated back into his bedroom window. He had to put a hand over his mouth, for he was panting so loudly. His bare chest was scratched and cut, and his pants were ripped. He took them off to discover a large cut on his thigh, probably caused by the glass in the cell window.

After a half hour, the camp alarm was turned off. Eventually, Jason got his breath back, but it would be hours before he stopped shaking.

═

The next morning, as Jason was getting dressed, his father came to see him. Jason grabbed his bed sheet and covered his cut and bruised body.

"What's wrong, son?"

Jason paused. He could not let his father see his cuts and bruises. "I'm naked."

"So?" Ray asked, looking puzzled.

"I am..." Jason said, trying to think of something to say, "I'm getting older now. I don't burst into your room, Dad."

Ray nodded and left him alone.

When Jason finally came out of his room, his father told him that he had to go into work this morning for a few hours and he would see Jason at the competition.

═

When Ray later arrived at the entrance of HMS *Tamar*, he noticed a photo of his son at the entrance to the guardhouse—one that was blurred and taken at night. Because he did not want to give Jason away, he asked who it was. The guard shrugged and gestured to another MP who came out to greet him.

"Hello, Lieutenant Steed. A boy has been seen sneaking around the base. He has been using the flight simulator and God knows what else he has been doing. He was arrested last night and put in a cell. He broke out. He broke this office window and a cell window. An MP is in the hospital with a broken nose, and another has a broken finger," the lieutenant replied, pointing at the broken window.

"Do you know who he is?" Ray asked.

"He spoke Chinese and gave his name as John Lennon. Ha! I will get to the bottom of it and track him down. When I do, he will be charged with spying, trespassing, damaging HM property, and probably assault charges."

Ray knew he had to try and cover this up. He would deal with Jason later. He told the lieutenant to sit down. "This could be a major embarrassment for you and your unit. Are you telling me that you could not hold a child of what? Nine or ten in your cells? That he overpowered all your guards and still managed to get away? What if this was a real spy from Russia? China? How will it make us look?"

The lieutenant fidgeted nervously. "Yes, you have a point. What do you suggest?"

"Destroy the pictures, clean the files, and reprimand your MP who let a child escape. Improve security on the camp and ensure no one else can break in and use the flight simulator. That thing costs millions." Ray's voice hardened. "It's pathetic that we have allowed a child to come and play on it like a toy."

The lieutenant agreed and slunk off after a sorry salute. Ray was furious. He phoned home, but Jason had already left for the competition.

He rubbed his eyes and then hung up, feeling strangely empty. *What kind of father am I?* he wondered.

Chapter Five

JASON HURRIED THROUGH HIS crowded neighborhood to the competition, already wearing his gi. Many of the local businessmen and women who had watched him grow up spoke Chinese to him and wished him well. He smiled back, but he was exhausted. He had bruised his head. His leg was in pain from the deep gash, and he was still worried about the previous night. What if someone saw him on the street and recognized him? But he was looking forward to showing his father his karate skills. This alone kept him going.

The tournament hall was packed with various karate teams from different dojos. Some press people and the local TV company were there. Jason found Wong Tong on the bleachers and wearily sat beside him. When it was Jason's turn to fight, he won each round, although he could see concern in Wong Tong's face. Jason knew his own heart wasn't in the moment. He kept watching the door, waiting for his father to show up.

The jujitsu group sat opposite Wong Tong's dojo. The grand master wore a black robe embroidered with gold dragons. Jet Chan, although older and much larger than Jason, was in the same category.

Jason wore a white headband with the colors of the British flag. Its sole purpose was to keep his hair out of his eyes. His speed and natural ability usually gave him an edge over his opponents. He had practiced his katas so many times that he could do them blindfolded. Besides, most of his opponents only studied one style, such as kung fu or tae kwon do. Jason would now face Jet Chan in the final round.

The two waited half an hour for their turn. Ray had still not shown up when Jason and Jet were called to the floor.

The two kids stood opposite each other. Jet Chan looked at Jason and smirked. "I have been waiting for this."

With that, Jet launched into a flying kick. Jason instantly stood aside and blocked it. Several hand strikes followed. When Jet Chan swept Jason's feet away from him, causing him to crash to the floor, he landed heavily on his cut leg. Jet pounced and held his fist inches from Jason's face. The referee raised his hand. It was one point to Jet Chan.

Again, Jason looked over at the door. *Where is Dad? He promised he would come and watch me. Everyone else has parents, grandparents, brothers, and sisters watching. Dad knows how important this is to me. Maybe he just doesn't care.*

The pair bowed and began again. Jason went through the motions of defense but failed to attack. In close contact, Jet head-butted Jason, knocking him to the floor. The crowd hissed. The referee shook his head and waved both hands. Jet was given a strike for a foul.

One more and he would be disqualified. Wong Tong ran into the ring with a towel and wiped the blood coming from Jason's nose. "You stop now. You no good today to fight."

Jason glanced at the jujitsu group, and they were all laughing. The grand master shook his head.

Wong Tong noticed and was furious. He grabbed his arm and led Jason to the corner, and for the first time in five years, Wong

Tong raised his voice at Jason. "Until now, I say nothing. Now I tell you. Grand master is no good. Wong Tong 'whips' him many years ago. Your father—he no good. He not come. You can't win for him. You can't win to prove a point to grand master. You can only win for one person: Jason Steed." Wong Tong continued, "So, you quit now and stop waste of my time or you win for Jason Steed."

Jason stood quietly wiping the blood from his face, looking at Wong Tong. He had grown very close to him and had never seen him so angry before. Most of all, he was annoyed with himself—the thought that he had upset his faithful teacher.

"Has it stopped bleeding?" Jason asked.

"Yes, you bleed no more. So, you quit or fight for you, Jason, no one else."

Jason nodded, energy coursing through his veins. He loved karate, and if his dad didn't, then so be it. He passed the towel back to Wong Tong. "Thank you," he said in Chinese, bowing his head.

The crowd fell silent as Jason walked over to his corner. He took off his headband and shook his blond hair across his eyes and then crouched into a fighting position. The referee wiped the blood from the floor and stood back. With clenched fists, Jason squinted through his bangs.

His adrenaline pulsed. All he could hear was his own heartbeat as he balanced lightly on his toes. Jet Chan was still smiling. The referee shouted "Go," and they both stood motionless. Jason moved forward to do a very basic tae kwon do kick. He knew how Jet would defend, but at the last second, Jason spun around and hit out with a punch he had learned from kung fu. The punch landed squarely on Jet Chan's surprised nose. Blood splattered Jason and the referee. Jet fell back to the floor with blood running from his nose. He thumped the ground in temper.

"Foul!" shouted the referee.

Jason was now also given a warning—still one point down. Jason looked back at Wong Tong and winked with a smirk on his face. Wong Tong nodded and smirked back.

Again, the opponents stood ready to fight. At the word "Go," a very angry Jet launched into a flying kick. Jason dove to the floor, rolling over and springing back to his feet with a return kick. Jet blocked the kick and tried to sweep Jason's feet away from him. Jason jumped clear and then sprang back with a high kick back, catching Jet's chest. The referee raised his hand. It was now one point each.

The next to score a point would win. The grand master looked on, annoyed. He stood with his arms folded and glanced over at Wong Tong, who smiled and nodded in delight.

Jason now attacked. He used tae kwon do, kung fu, and Shotokan. He even threw in some judo maneuvers to confuse Jet.

Because he found it so hard to defend against moves he had not seen before, Jet used his height and reach as an advantage over his younger and smaller opponent. He did not want to get in close quarters with Jason. He now realized that Jason was far too fast for him. They sparred for several long minutes. Jet desperately tried to keep Jason at bay. He could not see Jason's eyes hiding beneath his long bangs. They exchanged punch after punch and a variety of kicks. Jason's forearms became numb with the constant blocks from Jet's attacks. His nose had started to bleed again. His white gi was now splattered with his and Jet's blood. It became heavy with moisture as it soaked up sweat.

The excited audience stood up and cheered the two fighters on. The final fight in the competition had turned out to be a spectacular event.

Jet tried an illegal high kick to Jason's neck. Jason turned, and it caught his shoulder; however, he returned at lightning speed with a sweep of his own. Jet's legs were sent high in the air as he fell to the floor. Jason jumped on him heavily, landing his knee into Jet's chest. He punched at Jet's throat—a move that could have been fatal—but stopped an inch from Jet's windpipe.

The referee raised his hand and pointed at Jason.

The crowd erupted in applause. Wong Tong and students from his dojo ran into the ring. Jason gave Jet Chan his hand and helped him up. With a nod of respect, Jet then gave a bow of recognition to Jason.

His father may not have been there to see it, but that was his loss. Jason knew that he had won more than just a silver trophy.

═══

When he arrived home, Jason barely had the energy to push open the stiff front door. "Dad?" he called.

"In here," Ray barked from his room.

Jason found his father packing a suitcase. "Dad, look—I won the competition. I won this." He held out his trophy with a smile on his face.

Ray ignored him at first. The room went quiet. Jason was unsure what to expect. Then, Ray placed a folded piece of paper in Jason's free hand. He put down his trophy and opened a copy of the picture the MPs had taken the previous night. Ray looked at Jason and raised his eyebrows, looking for an explanation. It did not come.

Ray swung the back of his hand at Jason's face. Jason raised his forearm and blocked it, but his father's weight and momentum pushed Jason to the floor.

"You are fast," Ray muttered. He let out a long, deep breath. "Listen to me. You lied to me. You have shown me that I can't trust you. You have really disappointed me, son. I don't really care you broke in and played around on an assault course or that you broke into the flight simulator room. You're a ten-year-old boy. I would expect something like that. But why did you lie to me? Why did you betray me?"

Jason felt tears stinging his eyes. He opened his mouth, but the words stuck in his throat.

"We can't go on living here," his father continued. "I was going to tell you that I had planned to stay here full time and be home every night. I was offered a position at *Tamar*. However, now I have been forced to take another position, thanks to you. I can't risk you getting spotted by an MP. I have taken a new position on HMS *Ark Royal*. I will be away probably as much as I am now. It is based in Portsmouth, England. That's why I am packing. We leave for London in the morning." He bit his lip and shook his head. "You look a bloody mess. Take a shower and get to bed."

Jason was so exhausted that it didn't really sink in that he was actually leaving Hong Kong and everything he knew. His gi bottoms had stuck to his cut leg. His nose was hurting, and his arms and legs were bruised everywhere from the blocks he had made during the competition. The adrenaline he'd used for his fight had sapped every ounce of energy that had remained.

After a shower, he climbed out, slipped, fell on the wet floor, and caught his head on the wall. He felt light-headed, and he was unable to get up. Reluctantly, he called his father.

"Dad, Dad, I need your help."

Ray ran into the bathroom to find his son, naked on a wet floor, his leg covered in blood, unable to get up. He carried him to his room and bandaged his leg and cleaned him up.

"Are you all right now?" Ray asked as he sat him on his knee and hugged him. Jason looked into his father's eyes, tears coming uncontrollably.

"I promise…I really do promise, Dad. I will never lie to you again. I am sorry. I was scared and didn't know what to do. I did not want to hurt the MPs. I just wanted to get away."

Jason wept as he spoke, choking on the words. Ray wiped Jason's eyes and kissed his forehead and rocked him back and forth.

"Just be honest to me, son. We only have each other. I have to trust you—that's all I ask. If you do something wrong, anything, we will deal with it as a family. No one is perfect. Just be honest with me."

Jason had had no idea how much his father truly cared for him. Ray's own parents had never expressed themselves much, and it was hard for him to do the same. He continued to rock Jason back and forth. Deep down, although he'd never tell Jason, he was proud that his son had gotten the better of the MPs. He looked down at the shining, large silver trophy Jason had placed on the floor.

"I see you got a trophy. How far did you get in the competition?" Ray asked.

No reply came. Because he had now felt safe and comforted, Jason had fallen asleep.

Chapter Six

IT TOOK SEVERAL WEEKS for Jason to accept that he had left Hong Kong—his real home—forever. He spent most of those first few days sulking around the house and demanding to call Wong Tong so that he could at least say good-bye long distance. His father told him to keep quiet. Their move back to the UK was Jason's own doing.

Ray soon employed a woman named Mrs. Betton as a nanny and housekeeper. She was middle-aged and overweight and very bubbly. She let Jason have anything he wanted so long as he behaved, and she was also a great cook. Yet, despite how pleasant she was, Jason refused to get close to her. He had gotten close to Miss Watson and Mai Lee, and each time, he had gotten hurt when circumstances changed.

Jason made Ray's old room his own. He put his trophy up and bought some new Bruce Lee posters. He wanted a poster of Hong Kong to remind him of his old home, but he could never find one in the shops in London.

Ray enrolled Jason at St. Joseph's, the same all boys private school he had attended as a youth, just a short bus ride from the house. Jason, who could speak Chinese, English, and Japanese, now took French and Russian. He hated group sports. The idea of twenty or so boys running around a freezing cold, muddy field to kick a ball was not his idea of fun. He persuaded his adviser to allow him to take German instead. In return, he would join a local karate school and use this as his athletic credit.

With his father's help, he quickly found a tae kwon do dojo. As a ten-year-old, he had to join the fifteen-and-under group. When he got there, he discovered that the highest belt was blue and the average age was nine. The students did not believe Jason was a third Dan black belt until they saw his moves. He was surprised at himself: He was not happy with the discipline at the dojo. There were good facilities—showers, locker rooms, and even some weights to train with—but the atmosphere was too casual. Wong Tong would not have approved.

While in the locker room after the first day's session, a curly-headed man in his forties looked at Jason's black belt with three grades on it.

"Hey, kid, you shouldn't be wearing that belt. You have to earn that. Our instructor, Steven Coburn, has a third Dan black belt that took him years to earn. Take it off."

"It's my belt, sir," replied Jason, pulling his shoes and socks on.

"Like hell it is. Take it off or I'll take it off you," he shouted. Others looked up.

"It's my belt, sir."

The man walked up to Jason and held out his hand. Jason turned away and took his coat out of his locker. The man clicked his fingers and held out his hand under Jason's face.

"Tom, leave it," said a stern male voice. Jason turned. "I'm Steve Coburn, the senior instructor." Coburn was just over six feet. He had short brown hair and a bushy moustache. His dark eyes were so close to each other that it made him look cross-eyed. "Do you have anything to say, son? Whose belt is it?"

Jason sighed heavily, turned, looked at Coburn and then looked at the man whom Coburn had called Tom. "To earn a second or third Dan black belt, you need to look beyond what you first see with your eyes at first glance. Never assume anything. That is why you are stuck at a single Dan black belt. I have told you twice that it's my belt. Do you need me to tell you a third time or in another language maybe?"

The men were quiet. It was Coburn who spoke first. "You're new here. Let's start over. How do you like our dojo?"

"With all respect, sir, it's not for me. I didn't learn anything tonight. I won't come again," Jason replied, zipping up his coat.

"If you can move like you talk, I may make an exception and allow you to join the adult class. Would you like to try out?" Coburn asked.

Tom shook his head and walked off.

Without replying, Jason took off his coat, shoes, and socks and then followed the men into the dojo.

"Is this non-contact?" Jason asked. He wanted to be sure. He had heard that in Europe some dojos practiced actual contact and many pupils would go home with broken noses and black eyes.

"Always non-contact here," Coburn replied. Jason took off his headband and shook his hair over his eyes and then jumped into fighting position.

As they sparred for the next twenty minutes, a group gathered and watched in awe. They had never seen Coburn struggle to score points before. Here was this little blond kid with a funny accent and amazing speed and grace. Jason was easily the faster of the two, but Coburn was tall and had better reach. No one kept score of points, but it was an even match.

When they finished, both Coburn and Jason were covered with sweat. Jason was allowed to join the adult class. Coburn even offered to let him serve as an instructor whenever he would be out sick or had to be out of town for some reason. Wong Tong would have been proud.

=

At school, Jason couldn't seem to make friends. Many called him teacher's pet, as he enjoyed learning to speak different languages. He had to wear a gray uniform, white shirt, maroon tie, and school cap with a matching blazer jacket, all of which he hated and all of which he had to wear every day.

At the beginning of his second week, Jason went into the toilets during lunchtime. He heard a boy asking to be let go, so he rounded the corner to find three tenth graders holding a fourth grader down. They were trying to push his head down the toilet. Jason recognized the boy from his math class: His name was Scott Turner. He was brilliant at science, but he was teased like Jason was.

At first, Jason thought he should keep out of it, but the boy asked for help.

"Get away, blondie, or you'll be next," Wayne Parker, the gang leader, spat. He was a red-haired, plump boy with a face covered in freckles.

"Let him go, guys," Jason pleaded.

"Shut up." Parker stomped over to shove him. Jason caught Parker's arm, stuck his foot out, and threw him across the room. It was just a simple judo throw, but his head smashed against a sink.

"You are bloody dead, blondie," said a tall, skinny member of Parker's gang. He approached Jason and kicked at him. Jason caught his foot as it neared his face and twisted and pulled. It sent him down on the floor, landing on his back. He got up and ran at Jason, who replied with a perfectly aimed kick to the stomach. The boy fell to the floor, temporarily unable to breathe. "Let him go," Jason told the third gang member. He wasn't even winded. The older boy looked unsure at first. After another glance at his two friends on the floor writhing in pain, he decided to let Scott get up.

Scott straightened his tie as he passed Jason.

"Thanks. We better get out of here." The two boys left, leaving Wayne Parker and his fellow thugs to think about what they'd done. No doubt they wouldn't forget what had happened to them anytime soon, which was both good and bad.

═══

Scott and Jason had lunch together.

"You're the new boy, John Steed, aren't you?" Scott asked with a mouthful of cabbage.

"Jason Steed."

"Scott Turner. You know, they will want to get you back for that, and we could be in deep trouble for the damage to the sink."

"I didn't do anything wrong. He tripped," Jason said, smiling at his new friend. He had just lifted his fork when a voice called over the announcement system.

"Scott Turner and Jason Steed, report to the headmaster's office immediately."

"Damn," Scott sighed nervously.

"Come on. Let's get this over with. What's the worst they can do? Give us the cane? Five hundred lines? Detention?"

As they approached the headmaster's office, they could see an ambulance leaving the car park.

"Uh-oh," Scott said under his breath.

They knocked at the door and waited. The door opened to Mr. Griffiths, the headmaster.

"Come in, boys." He grinned.

Scott stole a peek at Jason, puzzled.

"No need to look so worried, boys. Now tell me the truth of what happened, and you will be all right."

In a halting voice, Scott explained how Wayne Parker and his gang had been trying to put his head down the toilet and how Jason had helped him.

"So, let me get this right. I don't for a second think bullying is correct. However, we have a way of dealing with things here. All you had to do is report it, but you thought you would start a fight, causing damage to school property. Your father will have to pay for the damage to the sink. You also sent one boy to the hospital and another home in serious pain. And the lesson learned here today?" Mr. Griffiths asked.

"If you get bullied, report it, sir," Scott replied.

Mr. Griffiths nodded and then looked at Jason. "You're new here, Steed. Your father attended this school. He was a great footballer. And the lesson you have learned today is, Steed?" Mr. Griffiths asked.

Jason paused. Scott was hoping he would give the same answer he gave.

"I would do the same again, sir. I didn't start the fight. Parker came at me. I just defended myself. The other boy tried to kick me in my face. He missed, and I kicked back. I can't stand by and watch a classmate get treated like that, sir, but I am sorry for the damage I did to the sink."

Mr. Griffiths turned his back on the boys and went to his desk. Scott whispered, "Just tell him you will report it next time to a teacher, please."

When Mr. Griffiths turned back to the boys, he held a four-foot-long cane. Jason was furious. He had done the right thing, and now he would be punished. He walked forward to Mr. Griffiths and thrust out his hand. This stunned Mr. Griffiths. Never before had a boy offered himself to be caned.

"What are you doing?" Mr. Griffiths asked quietly.

"You mentioned my father, sir. My father did attend this school. He is now an officer with the Royal Navy. If you feel he has brought his only son up wrong, that his son should not help a friend out in need, then I need to be caned, for I feel what I did is correct and would do it again." Mr. Griffiths was speechless as Jason continued, "However, sir, if it happened again, I would try to report to a teacher first."

Scott gave a sigh of relief.

"Yes, and so you should be sorry. Okay, I accept your apology. You may both go." As the boys were leaving, Mr. Griffiths said loudly, "Steed, I will be watching you."

Scott heaved a sigh of relief as they scurried down the hall. "That was close. Are you nuts? No one holds out their hand for the cane. Do you have a death wish?"

"Maybe." Jason shrugged. "That doesn't scare you, does it?"

"Nothing scares me but the food at this school," Scott muttered.

Jason burst out laughing. "Then, come to my house. My father's nanny will feed you right."

"You're on," Scott said.

From that day on, they were inseparable.

===

It was an unusually warm day in November when Ray came home unannounced. He found Mrs. Betton sleeping in front of the TV. She woke as he entered the room.

"Hello, sir. It's nice to see you. We didn't expect you. Jason will be pleased," she said, trying to wake herself up.

"Hello, Mrs. Betton. The house looks nice…thank you. Is Jason in his room?"

"No, he and Scott are out in the gardener's shed. They spend quite a bit of time in there. Crazy, if you ask me. They have this huge house to play in, and they spend time in that cold, damp place."

"Is Scott a friend?" Ray asked.

"Of course, you have not met him. Yes, he spends every other weekend here, and Jason spends the other weekends at his home. I hope that's okay. He is in Jason's class at St. Joseph's. I believe his father is a doctor. Seems like a nice family, although Scott does use a four-letter word too often for my liking. Let me get you a cup of tea." Mrs. Betton lifted her heavy body from the couch. Ray went into his office and through his pile of unopened mail.

"Here, sir, hot tea and fresh carrot cake I have just made," Mrs. Betton said.

"How often do you make this?" Ray grinned.

"Two or three times a week. I did have to hide it. Jason was eating it when he came home from school and then would not eat his dinner, but I have him trained now. *No* cake until after dinner," she replied, laughing.

"Thank you…it sounds like you are getting on well together?"

"Yes, he's a good boy. Never any trouble. Apart from—" She paused.

"Apart from what, Mrs. Betton?"

"I don't like to tell tales, but I don't like what Jason does with the tennis machine."

"What tennis machine?"

"He went on and on about this tennis machine. It spits out balls. You said to buy anything he needed, so I did. I thought he would use it for tennis, but he doesn't use it as intended. I think it's dangerous, but you're his father. You decide, sir."

Ray continued looking at his mail and said to himself, "Never any trouble? Then, what's this?" He had a letter from St. Joseph's school and a bill for the replacement of a new sink and plumbing. It came to sixty-five pounds. He looked out his study window and wondered what Jason and his friend were doing in the shed.

Moments later, the front door slammed open. He heard two boys' unbroken voices laughing out loud and footsteps running up the wooden stairway.

"In here," Ray's called from the study.

Jason walked back downstairs, tugging at his friend to follow.

"Hello, Dad, I didn't know you were coming home. This is

Scott, my best friend," Jason smiled, beckoning Scott, who walked up to the stern-looking man and shook his hand.

"Hello, Mr. Steed."

"Hello, Scott. It's nice to meet you," Ray replied. "Can you boys sit down please?" he asked.

They sat down on a large green leather couch together.

"So, what is this bill for?"

Scott and Jason looked at each other and shrugged their shoulders.

"It's from the school," he added.

"Oh, that's for the sink. Sorry, Dad," Jason replied.

"Yeah, Jason cracked Wayne Parker's head against it and sent him to hospital," Scott said. "Served him right."

Ray looked at Jason and raised his eyebrows.

"Dad, he was with two other boys, and they were bullying Scott. They came at me, and I defended myself. I did not start a fight." Jason knew only too well that he was not allowed to use his martial arts outside of a dojo.

"Okay. Is there anything else I should know?" Ray asked.

"No, that was the only mishap," Jason replied.

"I understand you are staying at my house for the weekend, Scott?" Ray asked.

"No, Dad, he is staying at our house."

Ray stared at Jason, suppressing a smile. His son was still just as strong-minded as ever.

"Yes, you're right. Sorry, Jason. You're staying at our house, Scott. I was going to take Jason out for a meal tonight. You are, of course, invited."

"Thank you, sir," Scott replied.

"Boys, what is the attraction to the potting shed?" Ray asked.

Both boys looked at each other and went slightly red and looked uncomfortable.

"It's our den, where we can hang out without adults," Scott replied.

Jason bowed his head.

"What do you do when you're hanging out?" Ray asked.

"We try grown-up things," Jason replied.

Scott's face went bright red. He looked at his friend in disbelief.

Ray smiled at the boys. "I was being serious. What do you boys do there?"

"We took some beer from the kitchen a few weeks ago and shared a beer. We bought some cigarettes too," Jason said.

"I don't believe this. Come on. Tell me the truth," Ray said with his voiced raised.

"Dad, I made you a promise. I would not lie to you. I am telling the truth. But we both only got halfway down one cigarette each. It tastes awful. I don't really like beer. I won't smoke or drink again."

Ray looked shocked. He sat back in his chair. He locked his fingers together and looked deep into Jason's blue eyes.

"He's right, sir," Scott chimed in. "The cigarettes tasted like garbage. And your beer, yuck, I think the sell-by date has passed. That tastes like garbage too."

"Well, Scott, what would your father say if he knew while you were here you were drinking and smoking?" Ray asked.

"I don't know, sir. Please don't tell him. He may stop us from seeing each other," Scott replied.

Ray smiled and nodded at the worried boy. "I was joking, Scott. I've been in the navy for nearly twenty years. It's not my beer. It was probably my father's. Because he died before either of you were born, I am not surprised it's out of date. I would like you to destroy the cigarettes and promise me you won't try them again," he ordered.

Together, both boys replied, "Yes, sir."

"Good. I'll see you at dinnertime then."

As they left his study, Scott turned to Jason. "Your dad is cool. I would have been in deep trouble with my parents for that. Why did you tell him? You could have said we were just hanging out. Have you ever lied to your father?" Scott asked.

"I did sort of lie once."

"What happened?"

"Let's just say hell will freeze over before I ever lie to him again," Jason replied.

"If you don't mind me saying, Jase, you don't seem very close to your dad. Why is that?"

"I don't know."

"Do you like your dad?"

"I love him."

"Damn, Jase, you didn't even shake his hand, much less hug him. You haven't seen him for months."

"I'd rather not talk about it, Scott. Come on. We better go and destroy the cigarettes and that nasty beer," Jason said, running back out the front door, only to be called back by his father.

"Yes, Dad?" Jason shouted back.

"Show me the tennis machine and what you do with it," Ray asked.

Jason smiled and ran back into the house. He went to the cupboard under the stairs and pulled out a large black box. "Scott, grab the box of balls," Jason ordered.

The two boys set up the machine on the front lawn. It spat out tennis balls at speeds ranging from 30 to 90 miles per hour. Scott loaded the container and ran for cover to the front door with Ray.

"Where's his tennis racket?" Ray asked Scott.

"He's crazy. He doesn't use a racket. Keep well back, Mr. Steed. You haven't seen anything like this. I don't know how he doesn't get hurt."

Jason turned the machine on to 70 miles per hour and random. He kicked off his shoes, socks, and T-shirt. Then, he took some deep breaths and walked away from the machine. He was in the direct line of fire and stopped when he was fifteen feet away. He raised himself onto his toes and stood at an angle to the machine. He raised his hand. Scott held the remote control and switched it on.

"What's supposed to happen?" Ray asked.

"Shhh," Scott whispered. He had been told before not to make a sound, for Jason was concentrating.

Bang! A ball flew out and launched directly at Jason's face. Jason swung his left arm up and hit the ball with his fist, sending it in the direction of Scott, who ducked. Another and another ball spat out. He spun around, blocking the balls that fired at him at all heights and directions. For several minutes, he blocked ball after ball. Eventually, he missed a ball, and it hit him on his left ear and knocked him back. Jason dove to the grass. Scott turned it off and ran over to Jason who was rubbing his ear.

"How fast did you have it?" Scott asked.

"Seventy miles per hour," Jason said, climbing to his feet and rubbing his ear, checking to see if he was bleeding.

"Then, that serves you right for showing off. You have never done over sixty before. Are you all right?"

"Yes, but it hurt like—" Jason paused when he saw his father approaching.

Ray looked at Jason and Scott and then at the tennis balls surrounding the area. He squinted at Jason's ear, now bright red, and then looked at his fists. Some of Jason's knuckles were split and bleeding.

"Why?" Ray asked.

"It's karate training, Dad. I want to get up to 90 miles per hour eventually. I can't get really hurt—just bruised. I love it." He was smiling and panting, dripping with sweat.

"Okay, but only use it when Scott is here." Ray patted his son on the shoulder and then walked back into the house without another word, shaking his head.

Chapter Seven

RAY TOOK THE BOYS to a very expensive London restaurant called Daphne's.

"Holy crap. I have seen this place on the TV. Mick Jagger, Elton John, and loads of pop stars use it," Scott whispered, grabbing Jason's arm.

They were shown to a table by a French waiter.

"Merci, monsieur," Jason thanked him. He and the waiter then spoke a little in French. The waiter looked at Jason's father and posed a question.

After he had taken the order, Ray asked, "What did he ask about me?"

"He asked if we were being taken out by our grandfather."

"Bloody cheek. What did you tell him?" Ray asked.

"I congratulated him on how observant he was," Jason replied, and for a few seconds, he managed to keep a straight face.

"Jason, what's the first thing French children are taught in school?" Scott asked.

"I dunno."

"How to say 'I surrender' in various languages," he said and grinned.

Jason laughed and then watched Scott as he placed the napkin over his lap. When he saw his father do the same, he copied them. Ray suddenly realized he had never taken Jason to a place like this before. He hadn't instructed him about manners since they'd visited Buckingham Palace. A wave of guilt washed over him.

Scott's head was twisting from side to side, trying to spot a celebrity.

"I want to join the Sea Cadets, Dad. There is a group not too far from the house," Jason announced to his father.

"That's a good idea, but you have to wait six months until you are eleven. Will you also be joining, Scott?" Ray asked.

"No way," came Scott's rapid reply.

"You will have to get your hair cut, Jason. You can't join with hair over your eyes," he told his son.

"I have an idea about that. I will go next week and find out about joining."

"You're not eleven," Scott interrupted.

Jason gave a smile and shrugged his shoulders.

"Jase, how do you stop a French tank?" Scott asked.

"Don't know. I give up."

"Just say boo," Scott finished.

Jason rolled his eyes.

═══

As a typical November night in London, it was raining quite heavily when they finished eating.

"There is no point to us all getting wet. I'll get the car," Ray said. He ran out into the night down the dark alley, his feet splashing in the rain. He was fumbling for his keys when from out of nowhere, he was struck on the head with a metal pipe, which knocked him to the ground. Pain shook through his body. He felt dazed, and for a moment, he had blurred vision.

"Quick, get the bloody keys, Ron," a male voice hissed in the darkness. Ray lifted himself up and could see the silhouettes of two men. They picked up his keys and tried shoving them into the door.

"Got it, Harry," the other one whispered as he unlocked the door. At this point, Ray was back on his feet, although he was still holding his wounded head. He ran over and pushed the man into his car. As the mugger fought back, both he and Ray fell. The second man, Harry, was now at the driver's side and kicked at Ray, catching his back. Pain fired through Ray's body, and he released his grip on the mugger. Then, he heard the scraping noise of the metal pipe as Harry picked it up from the wet ground. Ray quickly stood to defend himself, and the man swung the pipe at him. Ray caught it and wrestled with Harry.

Suddenly, a flashlight beam caught the three men fighting. It was one of the restaurant staff. The waiter ran back inside.

"Call the police. A man is being mugged behind the building!" he shouted.

Jason took to his heels, pushing the waiter out of his way. He ran down the dark street and around the corner. As he approached the men, he could just make out what was happening. His father was being struck again with the metal pipe. He slumped to the ground but was still conscious.

"Kid, piss off if you know what's good for you," Harry told Jason.

Ray looked up and saw his son running toward him.

"Jason, go back, go back!" he cried.

Jason's mind went blank, and his rage took over. As he approached, Harry swung at him with the metal pipe. Ray staggered to his knees, but Jason ducked and caught the pipe. He swept

Harry's feet out from under him. Harry crashed to the ground and let go of the pipe. Without a second thought, Jason struck Harry with the pipe across the face. Then, Ron came out of the car and tried to grab Jason. He missed, and Jason turned and lashed out with a kick, striking Ron's leg just above his knee, which instantly shattered Ron's kneecap. Ron fell to the ground, screaming in pain.

Jason's adrenaline was on overload. He pounced on Ron then. He landed on Ron's chest with his knee and used the very same move he'd used on Jet Chan. This time, however, Jason threw a full punch at Ron's face. The blow shattered Ron's nose, spattering blood on Jason's face. Ron stopped screaming.

Harry was up again and dived at Jason, throwing him across the wet stone road. Jason quickly turned and pulled Harry down. At lightning speed, he started to pound Harry's face with his fists. Harry was knocked unconscious in seconds.

Now on his feet, Ray limped over to Jason and put his hand down to pull him off Harry. Jason felt a hand on his shoulder, grabbed it, and then twisted it, pulling his father to the floor and landing him in a puddle of cold, dirty water. As he held his hand and bent it further back, Jason pulled himself on top of his father and pulled back his fist to strike.

"Jason, it's me," Ray gasped.

After he blinked several times, Jason stopped. He stood up and helped his father to his feet. His body shook violently as the rain washed the blood from his face and hands. Seconds passed before he realized how badly he'd hurt his dad's attackers, but he felt no remorse. He felt only coldness.

=

Jason and Scott sat in the hospital waiting room while Ray's wounds were treated. Eventually, a police detective came and sat opposite Jason. He looked the boy up and down. Jason felt self-conscious. His clothing was covered in blood after all. He looked at the detective, who had greased-down hair and smelled of cigarettes. He wore a long raincoat that was spotted with rain.

"I need to ask you some questions, son. I am Detective Johnson. Can you tell me what happened?" he asked.

Jason looked at his trembling and cut hands. He wasn't supposed to perform martial arts outside of a dojo, and he knew he may have gone too far. He glanced at Scott, worried. He did not really want to talk to the police and say something that would make it worse.

"He will answer anything you want, sir, but only when his father is present," Scott replied.

"And you are?"

"Scott Turner."

"Okay, Scott, I only need to ask him a few questions. I am sure he can speak for himself."

"Yes, he can, and he will once his father is here. He is a minor, and you can't question him without an adult." The detective nodded and reluctantly got up and walked away.

Jason looked at Scott and smiled at him in thanks.

At that moment, they spotted Ray limping down the corridor. He managed a grin. "Hi, boys. How did you like your night on the town?"

"Are you all right, Mr. Steed?" Scott asked, climbing to his feet.

"I will be fine, Scott. Just some cuts and bruises—thank you."

"The police wanted to talk to me, Dad," Jason said, looking worried.

"I will deal with them," Ray replied.

Detective Johnson reappeared. "Mr. Steed, may I question your son? I need to know what happened," he asked, blocking the waiting room exit.

"No, he's ten. What do you want to know?" Ray replied.

"Yes, sir, I can see he is ten, but we have two adults in critical condition. One man has a shattered kneecap, and his nose is broken in four places. The other man has a broken collarbone, nose, fractured jaw, and cracked ribs. How did that all happen?"

Scott gave Jason a pat on the back and smiled. Jason stared at the floor and held his breath.

"My son saved my life tonight," Ray said sharply. "He defended me and himself against two grown men armed with a steel pipe. They attacked us. I am a navy officer. It's my job to protect this country. It's your job to protect us from scum that preys on innocent people going out for a nice meal. Now, you can either arrest us or see me anytime with my lawyer. Until then, I have to get these two boys home to bed."

Detective Johnson nodded and reluctantly moved out of their path. Jason still didn't know how to feel during the long drive home.

===

The following morning, Ray walked into the kitchen where Scott sat eating toast and drinking hot tea with Mrs. Betton.

"Good morning," Ray said.

"Good morning," Mrs. Betton replied. "Are you okay, sir?"

"Bruised and very sore, but I am okay—thank you. I think I will go and check on Jason."

He smiled as he looked at the mess the room was in. Scott had slept on a folding bed. The sheets and blankets were sprawled everywhere, and socks, underwear, and shoes were scattered across the floor. Jason was sleeping under a sheet, still wearing his pants and socks. Ray sat on Jason's bed and gently brushed Jason's hair away from his face with his fingers. He looked down on the floor where Jason's blood-stained shirt still lay. Jason rolled onto his back and opened his eyes. Ray bent down and kissed him on his forehead.

"Are you all right, son?"

Jason yawned and stretched his arms, pausing to look at his knuckles. They were bruised and cut, and his hands were still blood-stained. Ray took his hands and examined them.

"I think I am, Dad. My hands hurt, but they will be okay."

"Were you okay last night, Jason?"

"Yes. Why?"

"The detective thought you did a good job, but you may have gone above and beyond what was needed. Did you lose control?" Ray asked.

Jason sighed. "Wong Tong taught me how to increase my adrenaline rush. It's the most powerful weapon a man has. When you hear stories of how a mother lifted a car off of her child or how a man being chased by a bull jumped and cleared a six-foot fence, that's an adrenaline rush. Controlling it is a learning experience. I am still learning, but I knew what I was doing. I never lost control.

When I jumped on that guy, I knew I was going to punch his face. It never came into my mind to punch his windpipe."

"His windpipe?" Ray asked.

"Yes, it can kill a man. I did not want to do that. I didn't want to send a nose bone into his brain, so I struck down. I was in full control…I did go too far by breaking his kneecap. Before you say it, yes, I did hit that guy more than I should have. I just couldn't help it. I just wanted to hurt them for hurting you. I never felt like that before, but I didn't have any intention to kill them—just hurt them. I'm sorry if I hurt you. I just felt a hand grab me. I was so high on adrenaline that it's hard to just stop."

"I was impressed, son. I am very proud of you," Ray said, pulling him up and hugging him. He then said the words Jason had never heard from anyone before: "I love you."

Jason pulled away to look at his father.

"Really? You love me?" Jason asked.

"Of course I do."

Jason looked down and said nothing.

Ray lifted Jason's face with a finger under his chin. "You never doubted that, did you, Jason?"

Jason looked at his father, and his sapphire-blue eyes filled with tears. He didn't reply.

"Why? How could you not know I love you?" Ray asked, looking stunned.

With his voice breaking and looking away, Jason replied, "You blamed me for mom's death. You said, 'The hospital should have saved her and not the kid.'"

Ray sat back, put his hands on his head, and said, "You heard that?"

Jason nodded. Ray took Jason's face in his cupped hands, wiped Jason's tears with his thumbs, and made Jason look at him.

"I loved your mother more than life itself. We were so happy when we knew we were having a baby. When she died, I was so mad at the world and everyone else. Yes, I did think they could have done more to save her. We will never know now—Yes, I did wish they had put her life first, Jason. I loved her. At the time, you were a stranger to me, but as time has gone on, you mean everything to me—look—" Ray said, passing him his wallet. Inside were photographs in a small plastic envelope.

Jason opened the envelope and found nine pictures of himself. On the back of each photo was written "My son's first birthday" all the way up to his ninth.

"I don't have a picture of you for this year yet, but I will get one before I go. I take these everywhere. I am very proud to show friends my very handsome son. Please believe me—I do love you and always have. I guess I never said it until now. That's not how I was brought up. My parents, your grandparents, were very conservative, just like Uncle Stewart. Sorry, Jason. I never knew you felt like this. I never knew you heard what I said. Can you forgive me?"

Jason hugged his father.

"Why did you never say anything before? You normally speak your mind," Ray asked.

Jason just shook his head.

They could soon hear Scott walking up the polished wooden stairs. Ray got up and told Jason that they would talk more later. Scott entered the room with a plateful of hot toast and jam for Jason.

"Mrs. Betton asked me to bring this to you," Scott said, looking at Jason's red, teary eyes. "What's wrong? Are you all right, mate?"

"I just need a few minutes to myself please. I will be okay," Jason replied, wiping his bloodshot eyes with his bed sheet. And he knew he would, even though Ray would return to Portsmouth and the *Ark Royal* the next day.

Chapter Eight

THE FOLLOWING WEEK, JASON joined the Sea Cadets. He was given a form to complete and to get signed by a parent or guardian as well as the instructions on where to purchase a uniform, and he was also told to get his hair cut. Mrs. Betton signed the form. Jason did not let her read the section stating date of birth, which he changed to 1962.

The uniform was black, polished boots, dark navy trousers, a white T-shirt, and a navy jacket. Cadets wore thick white belts and blue tunics. There was also a white sailor's cap or a small navy cap to wear with the blue shirt.

Mrs. Betton took him to get a uniform and to get his hair cut at Derek's, a small barbershop. Jason explained that he needed his hair short at the back and sides but wanted to keep his long bangs. They showed him how to use Brylcreem, a hair gel, to slick his hair back over his head. It seemed to work. He would only need to slick back his hair before he went to Sea Cadets, and the rest of the time, he could wash it out and wear it long over his eyes.

=

For the first time since Jason had left Hong Kong, he felt at home again. He loved everything about the Sea Cadets. They spent weekends learning about seamanship, boating, compass reading, Morse code, and general military procedures, which included marching and saluting an officer. Best of all, his unit had been invited to attend a summer camp in Australia next year. He immediately applied and found out that it would be on the HMS *Stoke*, an old frigate used for training purposes.

When he told Steve about his trip in August, however, Steve was not happy. It was the same time as the British Karate Championships. He had already entered Jason in the under-fifteen category, and he was certain he would win. He could then enter the European Karate Championships. If Jason's mind was in it, he could win that too. Jason and Steve argued for half an hour, but Steve still could not understand how Jason could let such talent go to waste.

But Jason wasn't interested in getting trophies. Steve informed Jason that he himself was entering the British Championships in the adult division. Plus, he expected to advance to at least the quarter final. Jason responded that Steve should not enter if he had already admitted defeat.

The pair never spoke of it again. Jason still continued with karate and continued to spar with Steve. Every now and then, when Jason would pull out all the stops and score an amazing point against his opponent, Steve would shake his head and say, "What a waste of talent." Jason also joined a Filipino martial arts school called Eskrima. It was a new style for Jason, but it gave him the opportunity to learn the art of swords, knives, and sticks.

Scott joined a science group too. He told Jason that computers were the future. They remained best friends, but with the Sea Cadets, karate, and science group dividing their time, they didn't have many days to spend together outside school, which was probably all for the best, Jason reasoned. When they grew up, they'd probably end up serving Britain in different ways in the Intelligence Service—or so Jason dreamed. Not that he ever mentioned as much to Scott.

=

It was a cold Tuesday the first week of December when Jason met Scott in the school lunchroom. Jason was already eating at an empty table.

"Where have you been? I'm starving, so I got mine and started," Jason asked.

"I put your name down next to mine for the Benenden Dance," Scott said excitedly with a mouthful of chips.

"Benenden Dance? What's that?" Jason asked.

"It's the Christmas dance. Every year, St. Joseph's goes to Benenden Girls' School for a Christmas party. It's a tradition. We have to wear a tuxedo. I've never been, but some of the guys said you get to smooch with the girls." Scott held an apple in his hand and kissed it, as if it were a girl.

Jason laughed so much he nearly spit out his food. "When is it?" he asked.

"December 18th," Scott replied.

"I can't go. I have karate that night."

"Crap, Jason. You go to karate twice a week. This is once a year. Don't you want to get close to some girls?" Scott asked, making movements with his hands of the shape of a woman's body.

"No, I don't really want to get close like that to a girl."

"I don't know if you and I should sleep in the same room

anymore," Scott teased. "Let me think of your two choices. One—you can grapple with a bunch of boys' bare feet all night, making strange noises. Two—you can join your best friend, have a great time, and dance with some pretty girls."

Jason rolled his eyes. "Fine. Now would you let me eat in peace, please?"

===

Scott's mother took the boys to a tailor in London's Savile Row to get fitted for a dinner suit. Mrs. Turner was a well-spoken lady with long black hair that flowed down her back. She chose a very old-fashioned store that smelled of mothballs. Suits, shirts, and ties hung around the wooden walls.

Jason asked the tailor what the difference was between the dinner suit Scott was buying and the tuxedo.

A thin man with an upper-class voice replied, "The tuxedo is an American-cut suit. It has thinner material and is expensive. They seem to be becoming popular but not worth the money."

"I prefer it. It looks sharper," Jason replied.

"Sir, maybe your mother had better look at the price first," the tailor replied.

He was going to argue and say she was not his mother, but for the brief moment, he liked the idea, so he said nothing. Mrs. Turner came and looked at the ticket.

"Oh, my, no, Jason. You don't want that. It's three times the price and just feel it. It's thinner material. No—get what Scott is having. That costs enough."

"Did Mrs. Betton not give you enough money?" Jason asked, feeling the suit.

"Well, she gave me a check, but I don't think I can spend that much, dear."

"Sir, may I call my nanny?" Jason asked the tailor. A phone was brought to the counter. Jason dialed home and spoke to Mrs. Betton.

"I found a suit I like, but it's very expensive. Can I get it?"

"You can get any suit you wish, but remember that you will probably only wear it for a few hours that night and it may not fit next year."

Jason thought for a moment. "If that suit's good enough for Scott, then it's good enough for me. I will get the same."

=

The night of the Benenden Christmas party, Jason made his way to school. It was a short bus trip he had now taken many times; however, it was 5:30 p.m. and dark, and besides, he was wearing a dinner jacket.

He noticed people staring at him as he climbed the red double-decker bus, so he went upstairs, and to his relief, it was empty. At the next stop, some kids a few years older than him got on and also went upstairs.

"Look. It's baby James Bond," said one youth who reminded Jason of Wayne Parker. He was almost as big as Parker but rougher-looking and scruffy. The others laughed.

"Tell me, Bond, where is one going tonight?" he asked, trying to sound snooty.

"To a party," Jason said quietly.

"I bet he goes to that fancy St. Joseph's. All the toffee noses go there. Do ya?" another asked.

Jason felt uncomfortable. He had another three stops to go before he got off, and traffic was not moving very fast.

"Yes, I go to St. Joseph's," Jason replied, trying not to make eye contact.

"Hey, Johnny, what ya think I would look like in a whistle like that?" the boy asked his friend. "Hey, Bond, let me try on the jacket. Give us a try," he ordered.

Jason stood up. He was trapped in his seat and could not get to the aisle.

"It won't fit you, and I get off here," Jason said.

"Don't lie, baby Bond. You said you go to St. Joseph's. Do you think I'm bloody stupid? Sit down," he shouted.

Jason sat back down and moved toward the window, trying to ease farther away.

"What money you got on ya?" the boy asked.

Jason ignored the remark and stood up again. An alarm bell went off in his brain. It was only going to get worse now that they had asked for money.

"I'm getting off now. Excuse me, please."

"You get off when I say you get off. Empty your pockets," he demanded.

"You probably won't believe this, but I have to warn you. I am a martial arts expert. I will use it to defend myself. Now, if you start anything, it's your responsibility."

The three boys laughed and made kung fu noises and waved their arms about.

Suddenly, one made a grab for Jason's bowtie. Jason caught his hand and twisted it. The kid screamed.

"I warned you. Tell your mates to back off or I will break it," Jason said, but his warning did not work. Another kid jumped over the seat and swung Jason. He ducked, but it still caught the side of his face because Jason was still trapped between the seats.

The first youth bit into Jason's hand until he let go. More punches followed. Many were blocked, but now and again, a few caught Jason's face. As they continued to pummel him, Jason jumped up and grabbed the metal handrail, lifted himself free from the seats, and kicked out at them.

Once he got to the aisle, he could protect himself. He hit out at one and caught him on the chin, knocking him back. As he did this, the black youth dove on him, knocking him to the floor. Jason knew he had to get up at all costs. Left on the floor, he would get kicked and seriously hurt.

Jason drove his two fingers into the black youth's eyes, causing him to scream in pain. He got out from under him and ran down the stairs. While the bus was still moving, Jason leapt off the back of the bus into the road. The three bullies did not follow.

He had to run the rest of the way to school. He was now late, sweating, and his suit was dirty from his rumble on the bus floor. He looked up at the two buses in the parking lot and saw Scott waving to him.

As he tried to enter the bus, he was stopped by Mr. Griffiths.

"Out of the question, Steed. You can't go as a representative of St. Joseph's looking like that. I am sorry, but I can't let you go," Griffiths told Jason.

"Can I go in the school and clean up, sir?" Jason asked.

"No, we are late already. It's an hour's drive to Kent. We have to leave now. Sorry, but you should have thought of this before you did whatever you did to get into this mess. I am sure your father did not send you looking like this." He then noticed Jason's hands. "Good heavens. Have you been fighting again? Go home, Steed."

"But, sir, I was attacked on the way. I had to get off the bus and run the rest of the way."

"Attacked, boy? Where?" Griffiths asked.

"On the bus, sir," Jason said, tucking his shirt in and trying to put his collar straight.

Scott made his way back to the front of the bus and came down the steps. "Sir, you can't leave him here."

"Get back to your seat, Turner, or you will join him."

"Okay, but if you throw me off, I wonder how our parents will feel when they hear you sent two ten-year-olds off the school bus at night in the dark. It will be worse when they hear one had already been mugged. My parents won't be back here to pick me up until midnight, but if you think it's safe to leave us here, I will stay off and join Jason," Scott protested.

Griffiths paused. He examined the boys in front of him while he tried to work out how to proceed.

"Clean him up. I shall want to see you both in my office in the morning," Griffiths continued.

Jason followed Scott onto the bus.

"Crap, mate. What happened to you?" Scott asked as they slunk down into the back row.

"Some teenagers thought I looked like a baby James Bond," Jason said, licking his fingers and trying to wash the cut above his eye.

"How many were there?" Scott asked.

"Three."

"Just three teenagers did this?" Scott asked, frowning.

"What do you mean just three? I'm not superman. I was lucky to get away," Jason muttered.

"I didn't mean it like that—sorry. It's just that it looks like they got a few good punches in. To me, you are invincible."

"Well, I'm sorry to let you down. I will try bloody harder next time."

"Hey, okay, I said sorry. I mean it—sorry. I am glad you're not badly hurt."

Jason nodded and swallowed. "Scott—Thanks, mate. Thanks for giving it to Griffiths," he murmured.

"Yeah, but we could be in hell tomorrow. Give me your jacket. I'll see if I can brush the dirt off it."

=

Benenden Girls' School was set deep in the Kent countryside. As the two buses pulled into the large gravel courtyard, Griffiths instructed the boys to be on their best behavior. He paid particular attention to the older boys and told them that if they danced, their hands could drift onto the girl's waist but no lower. There was to be no contact beyond that.

When Jason and Scott climbed off, Griffiths went to grab Jason's shoulder to take a look at him. Jason's instinctive reaction was to knock the hand away, and he did with a lot of force.

"Sorry, sir. I just saw a hand grabbing at me," Jason said.

A stunned Mr. Griffiths rubbed his hand. "Dangerous, Mr. Steed. Very dangerous. You need to control that. Let me look at you. Okay, you look better. Enjoy yourselves."

As they walked toward the main entrance, Scott's eyes were wide open in amazement. "Whoa, you hit Griffiths," he said, laughing.

"I didn't hit him. I just knocked his hand away, but you're right, mate. Whoa." Jason grinned.

They entered the huge double doors of an old mansion. The house had been converted into a school over a hundred years ago. The large entrance hall had a Christmas tree that stood over twenty feet tall, which was lit up with twinkling lights. Colored tinsel surrounded the tree, winding up like a mountain road to the top, where a brightly lit silver star had been placed. As the boys from St. Joseph's walked in, they gaped at the tree.

"Wow, look at that," some remarked.

Music could be heard as they entered the main dining room. Jason went to the bathroom to try to clean up some more. He looked at himself in the mirror and noticed some bruising on his face. He pulled his blond fringe of hair over his cut.

Most of the girls were in groups around the room. A small group of six girls danced in the center. Decorations stretched across the huge ceilings. The picture lights shone dimly on the many paintings around the edges of the room. The only other lights came from the DJ's disco ball. The purple glow of an ultraviolet light lit the dance floor, which was followed by some flashing colored beacons.

Scott made his way to the large food table that was spread across the far end next to the DJ booth. The boys dared each other to go over and ask a girl to dance. The girls looked the boys up and down and giggled to themselves.

Jason caught a girl staring at him. She was blond, not terribly tall, and she was whispering in a redhead's ear.

"I think they fancy us," Scott muttered, nudging Jason.

The girls both smiled at Jason and Scott. Without thinking, they both approached.

"Hello. I'm Susan, and this is my best friend, Catherine," the redhead said.

Jason looked at Catherine, and she looked back; however, neither of them said anything. They just stared at each other, trying to think where they had met before. Scott held out his hand and shook Susan's.

"Hi, Susan. I am Scott, and this is—" and then he was interrupted.

"You're Jason," Catherine said, walking forward. Scott's and Susan's mouths fell open.

"You know him?" Susan cried.

Jason smiled. "Hello, Catherine. Can you swim yet?"

"But…but you're Princess Catherine," Scott stammered. "You know each other?"

"Dance?" Jason asked Catherine, taking her hand.

The couple danced to Slade's "Merry Christmas." When that finished, the DJ slowed things down and played Donny Osmond's "Puppy Love."

"I thought you lived in China or Japan?" Catherine asked.

"No, it was Hong Kong. I live here now. You've grown since I last saw you. You never answered my question. Can you swim now?"

"Yes, thank you. I had lessons immediately after my party. You bought me my armbands." Catherine looked into Jason's sapphire-blue eyes. She leaned forward and put her head on his shoulder as they danced to the slow music.

"Why is everyone looking at us?" Jason whispered.

Catherine lifted her head. "That's normal. If you want to dance with me, you have to learn to ignore it."

"Really?"

"I suppose I am used to it," Catherine laughed.

When the music stopped, Jason asked, "Can I see you again? I mean…alone? Maybe go to the cinema? That new film *Herbie* is out—the one about that magic Volkswagen Beetle."

"It's not that easy, Jason. I can't just jump on a bus and go to the cinema with you."

"Why not?"

"Can you see that man over there by the door?"

"You mean the guy who keeps giving me the evil eye?"

"Yes," Catherine said, laughing. "He's a policeman in the Secret Service. Everywhere I go, he goes."

"You mean he would have to come too? Well, I am not paying for him to get in," Jason joked.

Catherine roared with laughter. "I have to go now. It was lovely to see you again."

They walked out together holding hands. Many eyes followed them to the door. A car was outside waiting for her.

"Are you having Christmas with your family?" Catherine asked.

"No, my father is away. I'm going to Scotland to stay with my grandparents," Jason replied.

The policeman interrupted, "We have to leave now, miss."

"I am going to Scotland too. We stay at Balmoral every year.

We are having a Boxing Day ball after Christmas. Would you like to come?" Catherine asked.

"Miss, we have to go now. Our car is blocking the exit," the policeman said.

"Yes, I will ask my grandfather to take me," Jason said.

They reached her car, and the policeman opened the door. Catherine climbed into the back but came out again, much to the annoyance of the policeman.

"What's your phone number?" Catherine asked. She wrote it on the back of her hand.

"Miss," said the police officer in a loud voice.

Catherine got back in the car and shut the door. Then, it pulled off and stopped after just six feet. Catherine jumped out and ran up to Jason. She gave him a kiss on his cheek and turned away to go. Jason caught her hand and pulled her toward him.

"That's twice you have done that," Jason said, smiling. He leaned forward and kissed her slowly back on her soft red lips, ignoring the hundreds of eyes that were watching.

"Steed, I believe her driver's waiting," Mr. Griffiths huffed from behind. They parted, and her car sped off, leaving a cloud of exhaust fumes.

In a daze, Jason climbed onto the bus and found Scott, who had saved him a seat. As he sat down, an older boy sitting behind them teased Jason. "Did you use your tongue?" he asked.

Scott scowled and turned around. "Grow up, David. Is this the first time you have seen someone kiss a girl? You need to get out more."

Jason pulled him back down in the seat.

"Watch your mouth, Turner. You want to say that to me again," the boy shouted.

Scott jumped up again. Once more, Jason pulled Scott back down in the seat. He glared at Scott and shook his head to say no.

"Why? Is he your boyfriend?" David said, now standing.

The boy sitting next to David grabbed him and whispered, "That's Jason Steed. He's the fifth grader that split Wayne Parker's head open. I don't think you want to mess with him. He's a black belt in karate."

David stayed sitting after that.

"Don't ever do that again," Jason said quietly to Scott. "I only use karate in self-defense. Don't ever think just because you are with me you can run your mouth off."

"Sorry, mate. I was trying to stick up for you."

"I know—thanks—but we will get into less trouble if we don't say anything."

Already Scott's mind was racing elsewhere with the excitement of the evening. "Jase, Susan was great. We kissed outside! I can't believe I just did that and that you knew Catherine? And she's a bloody princess—wow. You have to be careful, mate. You will get sent to the tower if you fool around with her."

━━

The minute Scott's father dropped Jason off at home, he ran straight past Mrs. Betton to the phone.

"I've got to call Grandfather," Jason told her.

"Jason, it's just past midnight. You can't call him now. Wait until the morning," Mrs. Betton said.

"It's urgent, Mrs. Betton," he replied, already dialing. It rang and took a while before it was answered.

"Hello," came a familiar-sounding Scottish voice.

"Gran, I have been invited to a Boxing Day ball at Balmoral. Can Granddad take me?" Jason asked.

"Jason? Is that you? Do you know what time it is? We were asleep in bed."

"Sorry, Gran. I just got home. Can I go?"

"Jason, it's going on midnight. Where have you been? Why are you not in bed?"

"I was at a school Christmas dance, and I met a girl. Please, can I go?"

"Your grandfather's asleep. If you want a favor, maybe it would be better to ask him in the morning."

"Okay. Sorry if I woke you. I'll call in the morning. Goodnight, Gran. Love you," Jason replied.

"Did I hear right? Balmoral?" Mrs. Betton asked.

Jason nodded, and a huge grin stretched across his face. He ran up the stairs two at a time to his bedroom.

Half an hour had passed, and Jason was still not asleep when the phone rang. Jason jumped out of bed and ran down the dark stairway in his pajamas and picked up the phone.

"Hello, Steed residence," Jason spoke quietly. No reply came from the phone.

"Hello? Is anyone there?" he asked again.

"Is that Jason?" a soft voice said.

"Catherine? Hi, I didn't think you would call tonight."

"Oh, sorry if it's too late," Catherine responded.

"No, no, it's never too late for you to call. Thank you."

"Can you come to the Boxing Day ball?" she asked.

"Yes, I already phoned my grandparents. It's 95 percent certain I can go."

"Your grandfather will take you?"

"Well, put it this way. I am his only grandchild, and he won't want me miserable over Christmas."

"I've got to go. Someone's coming. Bye." The phone went silent, and Jason put down the receiver. He skipped back up the stairs to bed almost flying.

=

The following day did not go as well as Jason had hoped. His grandfather told him it was a two-hour drive to Balmoral and the ball started at 7:00 p.m. and didn't finish until midnight. What was he to do?

The answer came in the form of a phone call from Catherine in the afternoon.

"Jason, Mummy has agreed to let a friend stay the night. Your grandfather can pick you up the next day."

Chapter Nine

AT THE END OF a restless nine-hour train ride from London to Glasgow, Jason's grandparents picked him up from the station. He asked if his dinner jacket could be hung as soon as they got home so that it would be ready for the ball.

His grandmother roasted a turkey for lunch, and they ate it with steamed carrots, roasted potatoes, and spring greens, probably frozen but brightly colored. She made a Christmas pudding and served it with Cornish clotted cream. Jason discovered a fifty-pence piece coin in his meal. He was embarrassed and did not want to hurt his grandmother's feelings, so he took it out of his mouth when he thought they were not watching.

His grandfather laughed. "Och, you found it. That's going to bring you good luck, laddie." Jason had no idea what he meant. He had never before eaten a traditional British Christmas meal.

The cottage was old and full of old furniture. An upright piano stood along the back wall of the living room. A faded shawl of burgundy velvet had been tossed over the top, which was now covered with Christmas cards. They also had an old cat called Nibbles. That first night, the cat crawled onto his bed and stayed, purring and kneading his top cover with its front paws.

He slept in his mother's old bedroom, arrayed with her trophies and medals as well as framed newspaper cuttings of her Olympic Games medal and other competitions she had won. In the dresser, he also found some old school yearbooks of hers and fell asleep dreaming of what she must have been like as a child.

═

The day after Christmas, Jason Macintosh drove his grandson to Balmoral. They approached the magnificent valley of the River Dee, rising high in the Cairngorm Mountains that ran east to its mouth at Aberdeen. Jason looked in awe at the spectacular scenery. Balmoral Castle was surrounded by over sixty thousand acres of the world's most rugged scenery.

"Just think. My grandson going to a royal ball and staying over-night as a guest," he announced proudly.

Jason squirmed in his dinner jacket because he was nervous and because he hated getting dressed up. In his clammy palms, he clutched a small bunch of flowers his grandma had given him for Catherine. His knuckles were white by the time they pulled up to the gate.

"Hello, sir, may I have your name?" a policeman asked.

"I'm just dropping my grandson off. Jason Steed. He is a guest of Princess Catherine," Mr. Macintosh announced proudly.

"We have Princess Catherine's guest listed as a Miss J. Steed?" the policeman asked.

Jason frowned. "Do I look like a miss?"

The policeman cracked a smile and then quickly regained his professional demeanor. "No, sir, it's probably just a mistake. Please go in. They will direct you where to drop him off."

They drove slowly up to the castle. Jason's eyes widened as he grabbed his bags and climbed out of the car. He doubted he could count all the turrets and windows and chimneys if he tried. "Thanks, Granddad," he murmured. "See you tomorrow afternoon about 5:00 p.m." He was barely aware of the car speeding off.

A doorman in a military uniform asked his name.

"Jason Steed. You probably have me down as Miss J. Steed." His face flushed slightly.

"Yes, sir, we do. Our apologies. Please go in."

Jason entered and paused in a long hall. An elderly woman wearing an elegant business suit and pearls approached with a list.

"I am Mrs. Crammer, Her Majesty's secretary. Are you here with your parents, sir?" she asked.

"No, ma'am, I am a guest of Princess Catherine. You probably have me down as Miss J. Steed. But as you can see, I am not a miss," Jason said, struggling not to blush.

"Oh, that was me." She twisted her lips in a thin smile. "I am sorry. I just assumed you were a friend of hers from school."

"Can I put my bag somewhere please?"

"Yes, I will take it to Catherine's room." She also snatched the flowers from his hand.

"Where do I go now?" Jason asked, looking around the great hall.

"You will see the ballroom on your left. Just follow the music." With a stiff wave, she vanished up the staircase.

Jason took a deep breath and strode toward a massive archway where the sound of a string quartet and voices trickled out. To his horror, the queen herself stood to his right as he entered, holding her hand out to him. She was dressed in a white evening gown with a sparkling tiara.

"Hello," she said and shook his hand, and Jason bowed his head.

"Hello." He had forgotten what to say, but his bow seemed to work. Then, the duke held out his hand.

"Hello, sir. It's nice to meet you again," Jason said.

"Likewise, young man," the duke said, although Jason doubted very much the kindly old officer remembered.

At last, Jason had passed that official welcome, and at that very moment, he spotted Catherine across the room. His breath caught in his throat, and he almost didn't recognize her. She wore a tight-fitting black dress with her blond hair tucked into a small silver and diamond tiara, and she also donned a pearl necklace and some delicate makeup. Their eyes met. She smiled at him. At least now he knew it was the same girl as she swept across the dance floor to greet him.

"Jason, you made it. We are going to have such great fun," she whispered, clasping his hand.

"Hello…You look—" he paused. "Nice…but different."

"Different?" she asked.

"You look grown up but beautiful. I had some flowers for you. A lady took them off me," he muttered.

"Are you all right, Jason?" she asked.

"I'm okay. Why?"

"What happened to the confident Jason Steed I was expecting?" she teased, walking toward the corner.

He managed a smile. "This is a lot different than a school dance. It's huge and scary."

Catherine kissed his cheek. From that moment on, he could barely remember a thing about the evening.

=

At well past ten o'clock, as the guests were leaving, Catherine took Jason through the very many corridors and stairways for a tour of the castle.

"This is our wing. That's Cuthbert's room, Henry's, Louise's… and this is my room."

She took Jason's hand and led him across the threshold. Like the rest of the house, it had cherry-wood-paneled walls with high hung oil paintings and deep-red velvet curtains. There was one difference, namely two large posters—one of Jimmy Osmond and one of all the Osmond brothers. Both were hung above her bed at slightly crooked angles.

"Look, those flowers in the vase. That's what I brought you," Jason said. His face turned red again. The red carnations suddenly looked cheap and garish compared to everything else in the room—except the boy band posters. Still, she walked over and inhaled deeply, closing her eyes.

"They smell wonderful," she said.

He blinked, smiling. "So…Jimmy Osmond?"

"Yes, he's great. Do you like him?"

"His song was good, but his voice is a bit squeaky."

The truth was that Jason hated the Osmonds, but if Catherine was nice enough to lie about the flowers, the least he could do was lie in return. And that set the tone for the rest of the night. They sat on Catherine's bed with their shoes kicked off, smiling and laughing and telling pleasant little lies on each other's behalf, until they both nodded off to sleep.

——

Catherine and Jason awoke late the next morning, and after they awkwardly took turns washing up in the bathroom, they joined the royal family for breakfast. When they entered the room, it went quiet. The table was full of everything Jason could possibly wish for: smoked haddock, kippers, bacon, eggs, sausages, tomatoes, toast, marmalade, jams, cereals, grapefruit, fruit juice, tea, and coffee. They sat down next to each other among some empty seats at the far end away from the others. Jason was still a little nervous of the queen, especially because his clothes were rumpled and they were all dressed formally again.

"Where did you two meet?" Louise asked from the other end.

"You don't recognize him?" Catherine said, grinning.

"Should we?" Cuthbert asked.

"Yes, you all should. This is Jason Steed. Without him, I would have drowned."

"You're the little boy who pulled Cath out of the fish pond," Henry said with a large smile.

"How did you meet up again?" Louise asked.

"Jason attends St. Joseph's. We met at the Christmas dance," Catherine answered.

"Oh, how sweet," Louise said.

"I thought you lived in Hong Kong?" Cuthbert asked.

"I moved here this summer," Jason replied.

"Do you like being back home, Jason?" the duke asked.

"I don't consider England home yet, sir. I was born in Hong Kong. That's home to me, but I do like living here now."

"Do you have an older brother, Jason?" Louise asked, smiling at Catherine.

"No, he is an only child, and he's too young for you," Catherine laughed back.

Nobody said a word after that, but Jason couldn't help noticing how the queen kept eyeing the two of them. She didn't look terribly pleased either. But maybe royalty never did.

=

After breakfast, Catherine took Jason to a massive book-lined room with a huge fire burning in a limestone fireplace. They sat down on the sheepskin rug and watched the flaming wood crack and spit. Catherine retrieved *Great Expectations*, a new book she had received for Christmas.

"I just got this. Have you read it?" she asked.

"No, I have heard of it. I think they made a film about it, right?"

"What time is your grandfather coming?"

He smirked. "Not until five o'clock. Why? Do you to want get rid of me already?"

"No, if it was up to me, you could stay here forever. Do you think we could read this by five? We can take turns on chapters. I'll go first."

They both lay on the rug in front of the fire, reading the chapters out loud to each other. Every so often, they would stop for drinks and chocolate. Jason wondered if he were imagining the entire visit. How had he winded up here when only yesterday it seemed as if all he did was train at Wong Tong's? If it had been up to him, he might have stayed here forever too.

When his grandfather drove into the courtyard that afternoon, Jason's heart sank. He did, however, allow himself a little smile at how nervous his grandfather was around Catherine.

"Hello, you…you're Royal Highness Princess Catherine," the old man stuttered, holding out his hand. "I am honored—"

"I will only shake your hand if you promise to call me just Catherine," she teased.

"Yes, hello, Catherine. It's nice to meet you. Jason has spoken a lot about you."

She sighed. "I guess you have to go now. Let's go up and get your bag."

They walked into the castle, and Jason's bag had already been packed for him.

He chuckled. "Wow. Just like magic. I could get used to this." Out of the corner of his eye, he spotted the queen through the doorway. She was talking to the stable hand, surrounded by three corgis.

"Catherine, can you do me a big favor?" Jason asked.

"Anything."

"My grandfather—"

"Of course," Catherine interrupted, squeezing his hand. "I will." She knew exactly what Jason was going to ask. She quickly ran down the stone steps toward her mother.

"Mummy, Jason is leaving now," she said. "This is his grand-father."

The queen looked up. She was dressed in a long green skirt,

black walking boots, and a dark green hunting jacket. A brown head scarf covered her hair. She approached a stunned Jason Macintosh.

"Hello, Mr. Steed," she said, holding out her hand.

As he bowed his head, Jason's grandfather took her hand and said, "I am honored, Your Majesty. It's Mr. Macintosh. I am Jason's mother's father. Has he been…good?"

"Yes, you have a wonderful grandson. One enjoyed his company. I have been listening to him read this afternoon. You have to excuse me. I have to talk to the vet about one of my horses." With that, she marched off across the courtyard.

Mr. Macintosh beamed.

"Thank you. He'll never forget that," Jason whispered in Catherine's ear.

Jason and Catherine hugged. As they slowly parted, she leaned forward and kissed him on the cheek. The cold wind blew Jason's blond hair to the side. His deep-blue eyes lit up.

"Call me when you get back to London," he said.

"I will," she said. "I will."

As the car pulled away, Jason once again spotted the queen in the mirror, her face drawn in a tight frown, staring at her daughter, who was waving good-bye.

=

A week passed—then two. Jason returned to his old life: school, Sea Cadets, and karate. But there was still no word from Catherine. He sent her a letter and waited. A week passed before a reply came.

He received the letter on a Thursday. He had just eaten his

dinner and gone to his room to get his bag ready for karate. On his bed sat a letter from Buckingham Palace. His heart pounding, he tore it open.

Mr. Jason Steed,

We thank you for your correspondence dated January 15, 1974. It has been decided that in the best interest of Princess Catherine's education that you cease to have any contact.

We wish you well with your education at St. Joseph's.

Yours sincerely,

Mrs. Crammer
HM Secretary

For a moment, Jason sat on his bed, stunned. He left for karate still in a state of shock, trembling slightly. He felt sick to his stomach. *What did I do wrong?* he asked himself. It just didn't make sense. Everything had seemed so perfect.

That very night, Jason sent an invitation to Catherine for a party he was having for his eleventh birthday in March. If she didn't reply, he knew he'd probably never see her again, but so be it. He'd survived worse. It was time to bury himself in his training and forget about everyone and everything.

Chapter Ten

CATHERINE NEVER DID REPLY. That Easter, a few weeks after his birthday, Jason went away with the Sea Cadets for Easter to the HMS *Fishguard* in Cornwall.

The second day, they were taken to the assault course. First, however, they were shown a plaque in the trophy room, which listed the names of fifty of the fastest around the course.

"Steed, look at number twenty-two," a drill sergeant told him. Jason's eyes flashed down the plaque. Completing the course in eight minutes six seconds was Raymond Steed, his father.

"No pressure then, Steed," the officer wryly remarked.

As they walked around the course, Jason observed each section in detail. It was identical to the course in Hong Kong. The fastest time here was seven minutes twenty-four seconds. He knew he could smash that time, and he became determined to at least beat his father's time.

There were fourteen boys in the Sea Cadets. Jason was the youngest and the smallest, but he still had more badges for map reading, rope climbing, Morse code, flag reading, drills, first aid, and swimming than any of the others.

He was to run in position thirteen. Typically, the cadets finished in ten to eleven minutes. Many found the hand-over-hand rope the hardest. If you fell into the net below, a minute was added to your time. Plus, you had to climb another rope ladder at the end to get back up. So far, only one had gotten all the way through the hand-over-hand on the sixty-foot rope.

Jason started heavy breathing before he set off in order to fill his blood with oxygen. At the word "go," he ran up a slope and through a set of tires. The instructors were clearly bored of watching the same old thing and simply stood with their arms folded. However, when he came to the hand-over-hand sixty-foot rope, their mouths fell open. As he used one leg as a cushion and one leg as balance in midair, he started to push and pull himself along the top of the rope with both hands at a terrific speed.

At the end, he slid down the rope and jumped to the ground, rolling to break his fall, as if he had parachuted. The cadets were now staring in amazement too.

He now pushed himself faster, adrenaline rushing through his body. He imagined that he was being chased by gunmen. When he came to the twenty-foot rope net, Jason jumped and landed on one rung. He leaped again, and his light body pulled and kicked its way to the top. At the top section, most cadets cocked one leg over and climbed down. Instead, Jason put his arms over the other side, pulling his body over like a cartwheel, and rolled down in a tight ball.

The water plunge was a ten-foot-large concrete pipe submerged in cold, muddy water. Jason ran at full speed, diving straight in, and swam into the pipe. Unfortunately, he smacked his forehead on the rim, but he ignored the pain and imagined a shark right behind him, which gave him an extra spurt of speed. He now had to run to the finish line. As he was running, a concerned instructor ran toward him. Jason's face was covered in blood, but Jason waved him off and pushed ahead, diving for the finish line.

"Seven minutes ten seconds. Holy cow, Steed. You just broke the record!" the instructor shouted. "You—"

But Jason didn't hear the rest. Instead, he collapsed in exhaustion.

≡

When Jason awoke, he was in a hospital bed. A doctor was peering down at him. Apparently, he'd received eight stitches on his forehead and had stayed in the hospital overnight for observation. The doctor was a little concerned that Jason might have had a slight concussion.

For the next hour, Jason lay in the hospital bed, watching the nurses and patients coming and going. The whole base reminded him of his old home in Hong Kong. In the bed opposite him was a trainee officer who had broken his leg in a parachute training exercise. He constantly complained about not being able to smoke in the ward.

"Jason Steed?" a gruff voiced asked.

He turned to see HMS *Fishguard* Lieutenant Commander Hoskins.

"Hello, sir. Please forgive me. I have been told not to get up too quickly," Jason said, saluting.

"Gosh, you are young. They told me a Sea Cadet broke our course record. I was expecting to see a six-foot fifteen-year-old. How old are you?"

"Eleven, sir," Jason replied, slowly standing.

"Sit down, son. You don't have to stand. They tell me you have an ingenious way of crossing a rope. Would you share that with my drill sergeants?"

"Yes, sir."

"How long have you been a cadet?"

"Three months, sir."

"Has anyone told you to cut your hair?"

Jason then remembered they had bathed him as he had been covered in blood and mud. His blond bangs were now in their natural place and looked much too long for the navy. Jason used his finger and brushed it back up over his head.

"Um—"

"It's too long. Get it cut. You are the youngest and smallest person we have had in our sickbay. I am glad you are feeling well. Congratulations on your record. I hope to see more of you." He saluted Jason and walked away.

=

The following morning, Jason joined the rest of the cadets. They had a briefing on the day's activities. It was an hour's drive to Dartmoor, where they would hike up a hill and inflate two rafts and then ride down the rapids.

Drill instructor Evans shouted out the orders. "No tomfoolery. We already had one cadet spend the night in the hospital. We don't want anymore!"

All eyes turned to Jason.

"As for you, Steed, you will have to sit this one out. The doctor doesn't think you should participate in the rafting. I am sure you can find something to do here."

Jason bit his lip. He wanted to argue because he felt fine. Plus, he really wanted to go white water rafting, but his uncle Stewart had told him, "You must *never* question an order—ever." However, he could not hide his disappointment. Some of his fellow cadets even gave him a pat on the back. Jason watched them pile into two minibuses with equipment stored on the roof racks. As they pulled away, some of the boys sat in the back and gave a mock salute as a friendly tease. Jason hung his head. He couldn't see the humor in it.

With nothing to do, he shambled down to the center of the complex. A broad smile came across his face as he read the sign: simulator. He poked his head and looked around. Two pilots were using the equipment.

Jason watched for an hour. When they finished, a female controller called out, "Hey, kid, I guess you wanna try?" She was a red-headed Irish lady covered in freckles.

"Yes, ma'am, thank you," Jason said, climbing in.

"Wait. You need to be shown what to do. You will never get it off the ground."

"If they can, I can," Jason said, strapping himself in.

"Look, kid. It's not a toy. It's an expensive bit of equipment. Pick an airplane."

But Jason had already picked a fighter jet and began the sequence to start. The controller stared in shocked amazement.

Jason went through the preflight checklist, started the engine, and took off. Once the simulator was in the air, the controller talked to him on the radio.

"Ha! Okay, kid. How did you learn to do that?"

"Hong Kong, ma'am."

"Well, show me your stuff then, Mr. Hong Kong."

Jason spent most of the rest of the day flying all sorts of planes, including fighters and huge cargo carriers. He did crash once when he tried a simulated landing on an aircraft carrier, but apart from that, he performed as well as any pilot she'd ever seen.

"You're a natural, mate," she told him, patting his head as he left. "And by the way, I love your hair."

———

Back in London, Jason plunged himself into the final school term before the summer holidays. He was looking forward to going to Australia and joining the HMS *Stoke*—away from any reminders of Catherine. Ray had been away for five months, and he did not know when he would be coming back. It was finally warm enough to swim outdoors, and Jason spent any spare time he could in the pool. One afternoon while he was splashing around, Mrs. Betton hurried out with a breathless look on her face.

"Jason, phone for you. Your friend Scott."

"Can I call him back?"

"It's urgent," she shouted back, holding a towel.

Jason climbed out, shivering. The pool was forty feet long, and he insisted on the heating being switched off. Scott told him he was crazy, but Jason felt he could swim farther and faster in the cold. He also said it was training for whenever he would become a spy or marine. Mrs. Betton chased after him, wiping up the wet floor behind him. While he spoke on the phone, she dried his back with the towel.

"Hi, mate, is everything okay?" Jason asked.

"You are going to love me. Just say, 'thank you, Scott.'"

"Thank you for what?"

"Just tell me: Who is your best mate? Who do you love, and who is better looking than you?"

Jason rolled his eyes. "Right now, Scott, if you were here, I would thump you. Spit it out, damn it." Mrs. Betton smacked Jason across the back of the head with the towel.

"There is a fund-raiser tomorrow," Scott announced. "It's a charity event for the refugees of Jakarta. It starts at 10:00 a.m. I will come over at 8:00 a.m. We have to catch two buses."

Jason's eyes narrowed. He knew vaguely what was going on in Jakarta—a civil war had broken out. Many of the women and children from the main city of Bandung had been evacuated. Jakarta was also not far from Hong Kong, located between northwest Australia and China. The Chinese government had been suspected to be involved with the trouble, but nothing had been proven yet. The president of the United States, Gerald Ford, was having trouble with the Russians, and he could not get involved in a dispute with China, whom the Russians might side with in a power play. Consequently, it had been left to British Prime Minister Harold Wilson to negotiate peace in the region.

"A fund-raiser?" Jason finally asked.

"Yes."

"A fund-raiser? I'm coming over to your house right now, and I am going to thump you. I was training. Why would I want to go to a fund-raiser? I'd have to pay to get in!"

"It's being run by the pupils of a certain school."

Jason blinked. "What school?"

"Benenden. It's open to the public."

Jason paused and smiled. "Okay, yes, you are better looking than me, and I do love you. I won't thump you."

"Come over to my house anyway. I have something to show you."

=

Scott's bedroom was as messy as Jason's was tidy and ordered. His walls were smothered in posters of NASA spaceships. Models of rockets hung across the ceiling from fishing lines. He had a table full of bits of radios he had taken apart. Wires, batteries, and circuit boards were scattered everywhere. His bed was still unmade. His clothes from yesterday lay on the floor beside empty bags of chips and Coke cans.

On his dressing table sat a huge radio.

"Look," Scott said, proudly pointing at it.

"It's a radio," Jason said, frowning.

Scott turned it on. "It's not just a radio. I am now a 'radio ham.' I can tune into anything."

"Can you hear the police?"

"That's kids' stuff," Scott scoffed. "I can hear the police in New York. I can hear our military anywhere in the world. I can't talk to them, but I can hear them. I was listening to aircraft taking off in India this morning. I can talk to other radio hams across the world."

"It's fantastic. Just perfect," Jason said.

"Really? You are not just saying that? I thought you would think that it's boring technological crap," Scott replied.

"I do think it's boring technological crap, but it's perfect for you. Seriously—I'm not trying to be mean. I can't think of anything better for you. When I go to Australia in August on the HMS *Stoke*, will you be able to hear where we are?"

"The navy uses frequency FM 36.5, and I tune in all the time. I will follow your course."

"Just like a real spy," Jason murmured.

Scott arched an eyebrow. "Now you're getting it, mate."

—

The next day, after a two-hour bus ride, Jason and Scott arrived at the Benenden School. Jason's pulse raced the entire time, but Scott seemed oblivious to his nervousness. They followed the handmade signs to the sports field where the fund-raiser was being held. In the center of a group of stalls, the school orchestra was setting up to play. The tables had white sheets covering them. Students and their parents were selling homemade jams, and others were selling homemade cakes.

Jason searched the field for Catherine and finally spotted her at a table serving homemade lemonade. She was serving some adults, and Susan was also with her.

Scott spotted them at the exact same time and hurried to the front of Susan's line.

"Do your dancing partners get a discount?" Scott asked.

She looked up. Her eyes widened. "Scott! Hi. What are you doing here?"

"I was dying of thirst," he joked.

"Jason's not with you—?" She broke off in mid-sentence.

Jason shook his head. "What's going on?" he asked. The words stuck in his throat. "Catherine?"

"I can't talk to you. Susan will serve you," Catherine stated awkwardly. She pushed away from the table and scurried off behind the stalls. Jason chased after her.

"Catherine, please!"

"Jason, I can't see you. Please, just go."

"Why? What's going on?" He felt that same sickness in his stomach that he had suffered when he had received the letter.

"Look, I got really hurt last time."

Jason had no idea what he had done wrong, but he refused to give up. "How did you get hurt? In Scotland, you kissed me good-bye and said you would call. I got a letter from the palace secretary informing me to keep away! I have feelings too. Have you ever thought about how I felt? You knew how I felt about you. What did I do wrong? Am I not good enough for you now?"

Catherine turned her teary eyes away from him.

"I…I just can't see you."

Jason caught her arm and pulled her back.

"Jason, let me go," she told him, crying.

Out of the corner of his eye, he noticed a tall figure attempting to grab him. He turned and blocked the hand and retaliated with a waist-high kick into a man wearing a suit. The man fell to the floor, holding his stomach. With his free hand, he reached into his jacket and pulled out a gun. Before he could point it, Jason kicked it away, dove, picked it up, and then turned the barrel on the man.

A wide-eyed, open-mouthed Scott slowly chuckled.

"Put your hands on your head," Jason ordered.

"No, Jason!" Catherine shouted. "That's my bodyguard!"

"Oh—" said Jason, horrified. He took the gun by the barrel and passed it back to the policeman. "Sorry, sir."

The policeman climbed to his feet. "The party is over," he said, removing his radio. "You're in serious trouble, lad."

"I wouldn't do that if I were you, sir," Scott piped up.

The policeman sneered. "And why not?" he asked.

"Well, go ahead. Radio and tell palace security and your police department that you've just been assaulted by an eleven-year-old boy. You pulled a gun, and he got it off you. Then, when you were identified, he gave it back. Now, what if he was a real terrorist? You would not have gotten it back. It wouldn't look too good for you, would it? It's an argument between two kids. Leave them alone to sort it out. She is in no danger from him."

The policeman blinked a few times. "Are you all right, miss?" the policeman asked Catherine.

Catherine was sniffing and wiping her eyes. Susan had her arm around her.

"I am fine. We all are. Sorry if you got hurt, Roger," she told him and then looked at Jason. "I am sorry. I owe you an explanation."

The policeman nodded and put his radio back in his jacket. Catherine seized Jason's arm and led him across the field away from the stalls and tables.

"Mummy was not pleased that we slept in the same bedroom," she murmured. "She thought that J. Steed was a girl. I...I wanted them to think that so they'd let you stay, but the idea of me having a boy in my room all night did not go over well. And I argued and got banned from seeing you. It broke my heart. Sorry. I never thought how you would be feeling."

Jason swallowed. "I thought you hated me."

She smiled through her tears. "Hardly. I was impressed with what you just did to Roger. You and Scott make a good team. I thought we would all be in big trouble."

"Tell your mother you want to see me again. It's been six months. She can't still be mad. We will only meet in daylight and with your policeman. No more sleeping together." Jason paused, turning red. "In the same bedroom, I mean."

She laughed. "I will ask. *No*. I will tell her I want to start writing to you again."

"She won't send you to the tower, will she?" Jason joked.

"No, but she may send you there—if you do that to one of the security officers again."

=

Monday morning, Mrs. Betton dropped Jason off with his travel bag at the Sea Cadet HQ. There were sixteen from his regiment going. In total, one hundred and twenty Sea Cadets from all over the UK would be joining the HMS *Stoke* in Australia.

The trip was almost cancelled at the last minute because of the problems in Jakarta, but the admiralty agreed that it should proceed and that they would "watch" the situation.

On arrival in Sydney twenty hours later, the excited cadets were driven to the navy base. The *Stoke* then set off to the north-west coast.

They were split into groups of six cadets—twenty groups in total. Regiments were mixed so the cadets would learn to team up with strangers.

Jason was in group number nine, which had six cadets: John Leigh from Cornwall, age fifteen; Rob Matthews from *Stoke*, age fifteen; Jeff Wesley from Yorkshire, age fourteen; Jim Bloom from Bristol, age thirteen; Todd Johnson from Liverpool, age eleven; and, finally, Jason Steed from London, age eleven.

Each group was given a bunk room—tiny, cramped spaces with three wooden bunks on top of each other on either side. The bunks had a small mattress and bedding. At the end of the room was an open unit split into six sections. There were no doors on the bunk rooms, so privacy was nonexistent.

≡

When group nine arrived at their bunk room, the older boys— John, Rob, and Jeff—picked their bunks first. Jason and Todd were left with the bottom bunks. They introduced themselves and unpacked. Jim went to find the bathroom.

"You guys have gotta see this. You won't believe the head," he said.

The other five followed him. They all looked, open-mouthed, at the stainless steel toilets with no doors. There were also six showerheads on one wall, ten sinks, and twelve urinals—and no doors anywhere.

"No way, look at that. Everyone can see you taking a dump," John said.

"No privacy whatsoever," Jeff replied. "It's all right for them two," he said pointing at Todd and Jason. "They probably don't need privacy yet. You don't yet, do you?" he said, looking at Todd and Jason. The two boys shrugged their shoulders and walked back to the bunk room together.

"I guess we are going to be the butt of the jokes." Todd sighed.

"I am too tired to argue." Jason yawned. He'd been up for twenty-four hours straight. The bunks were not very comfortable, but within minutes, he was sound asleep.

Chapter Eleven

As much as Jason liked being on the ship, he found the smell by the bunk rooms hard to deal with. One hundred and twenty young, unwashed, teenage male bodies, who had been wearing the same clothes, shoes, and socks for over twenty-four hours in the hot weather, produced a stench. Combined with the oil smell from the HMS *Stoke*, it was nauseating. Jason had no appetite.

After they forced down some breakfast, the cadets assembled on deck. Instructors barked out orders on washing, requirements on keeping the bunk rooms tidy, and details on the "best group" competition. The winning group would get to take a flight in a helicopter to the navy base and the HMS *Ark Royal* and get awarded a merit badge. John was assigned as group nine's leader. The competitions were on Morse code, swimming, diving, sailing, map reading, and inflatable boat control. John noticed Jason's badges on his uniform.

"Hey, Todd, you can help us win some of these."

"I'm Jason. Todd is the guy from Liverpool," Jason said. "But of course I am going to help. I really need to win this and get the helicopter trip to the HMS *Ark Royal*."

"Really? Don't take this wrong, but I thought I had been given the short straw. Most groups have maybe one eleven-year-old. We have to have two of you," John said.

"I can carry my own weight and will help Todd. You won't

have to worry about us. Put me in any swimming event you can. Seriously."

═══

That evening, Jason and Todd were enjoying the breezy silence of an ocean sunset when a voice barked behind them: "You! Cadet!"

The boys whirled around. It was the captain of the ship, William Giles. Jason and Todd saluted. Jason was positive that Giles didn't remember or recognize him from his stay at his father's apartment in Hong Kong six years earlier.

"What's that on your head?" the captain asked. Jason's blond bangs had been caught in the wind and again looked far too long for the navy.

"It's my hair, sir," Jason said, trying to brush it back down.

He grinned. "Report to the sickbay. Inform them you have been sent for a haircut."

"Yes, sir," Jason said, saluting again.

"What's your name, cadet?" Giles asked.

"Steed, sir. Jason Steed."

"Then, you should know better, shouldn't you?"

"Yes, sir. Sorry, sir. I will go now, sir." Todd followed Jason down to sickbay.

"What did he mean? You should know better?" Todd asked.

"My father is the lieutenant commander on the aircraft carrier HMS *Ark Royal*. I'm sure he knows who I am now."

They arrived at the sickbay. Jason reported in and came out in less than five minutes, rubbing his head.

"Well, it does make you look a little older," Todd said, laughing.

"Really?" Jason said. "Good."

"Yeah, you could pass for nine now."

=

The following morning, the competitions began. Rob and Jeff won the Morse code contest, giving team nine five points.

The swimming event was next. The objective was to circle an inflatable raft that was 220 yards away from the ship and then come back. The first to touch the ship would win.

Captain Giles watched the event. A rifle was shot in the air, signaling the start. They had to jump or dive off the side, which was a daunting task for many, as it was a long way down to the sea. Jason plunged into the cold water. Instantly, a boy pulled ahead of him.

It turned out to be Colin Warden, a tall, fifteen-year-old from Cardiff. Colin kept his head down and only came up for air every two strokes. Jason fought back but couldn't gain on him, although a huge gap started to grow between them and the rest of the swimmers.

Jason did not want to finish second. He managed to swim up to his opponent's waist, but Colin's longer arms and legs kept plowing through the water at high speed. Colin's hand hit the side of the ship, and a second later, Jason hit it. Dejectedly, lungs heaving, he followed Colin up the steel rung ladder back up to the ship's deck. Colin was cheered and congratulated by his teammates. Captain Giles came over and shook Colin's hand.

"You were lucky, Colin. I thought that little blond kid was going to catch you," one of Colin's teammates told him.

Colin turned and nodded in respect at Jason.

"Team six gets five points thanks to Colin Warden. Overall, team six is now fourth. Team nine gets four points thanks to Jason Steed. Overall, they are now in second place," an officer shouted.

Jason's team cheered as he walked toward them.

Captain Giles called out, "Well done, Steed."

Jason turned. "Thank you, sir."

═══

After lunch, they were all called on deck. A boxing ring was set up in the center. In their teams, the cadets sat cross-legged around the ring. Captain Giles stood on the small top deck overlooking the event. A muscular officer climbed into the ring. He stripped down to a tight white T-shirt. His bulging arms were covered in tattoos.

"I'm Sergeant Brown. I am a drill sergeant and expert in unarmed combat. We have a small program to show you how to defend yourself in hand-to-hand combat. Okay, I need a volunteer to come and kill me with this." He held a rubber knife above his head. Two older cadets both raised their hands.

"Good, come up here, both of you. Name and team?" Brown asked the first one.

"Tozer, sir, team four."

"Okay, one point to team four, just for being a volunteer."

"Damn it, that's Colin's team," John muttered to Jason.

Tozer stepped into the ring, and Brown passed the knife to him.

"Okay, Tozer, I am a Chinese Jakarta rebel. Kill me."

Tozer stood wide-legged with the knife tightly in his hand. He jumped forward. Brown caught his arm and threw Tozer over his shoulder. Tozer fell heavily to the floor onto his back. Brown then placed his boot over Tozer's throat. The cadets went silent. They didn't expect him to get hurt like that. Brown helped the boy to his feet and told him to go back and sit down. Brown explained the mistake Tozer had made. Jason looked up at Captain Giles, who was smiling.

The other volunteer was David James. His team was given a point, but his face was a shade paler now.

"Okay, Mr. David James. Don't make the mistake Tozer did. Here's the knife. Kill me with it," Brown shouted out.

David was hesitant. He switched the knife from hand to hand and walked around Brown like a fox circling its prey. After one minute, he was still circling and had not attacked. To David's surprise, Brown attacked him. He went forward and swept David's feet away, knocking him to the floor. Brown jumped down, landing on his knee onto David's back. He then took the knife from David, who lay stunned, gasping for air.

Brown again addressed the cadets as David staggered to his feet and lurched out of the ring. "I know some of you are thinking I've been a little hard, but I can't teach you to hold hands. This is combat. It's not for sissies. It's bloody tough. Now, talking about sissies, who here has done some form of self-defense like martial arts?"

Jason could feel Captain Giles looking at him.

"Come on, there must be some of you?" Brown asked. Jason glanced up at Giles, who was staring directly at him. Jason looked away. A hand went up. It was Todd.

"Come on up," Brown told him. "You don't get a point, as you didn't volunteer, but come in and tell me what grade you are." Todd made his way through the cadets and climbed into the ring.

"I have a brown belt in jujitsu, sir," Todd said anxiously.

Brown shook his knees back and forth and wrung his hands, pretending to be nervous.

"Oh, we have a brown belt karate expert—help!" Brown said, getting lots of laughs from some of the others. "I don't mean to knock you. What's your name?"

"Todd, sir."

"Okay, Todd, I don't mean to knock you personally, but that stuff is just a form of dancing. It won't protect you or save you. Don't you agree?"

Todd paused before he said, "No, sir, I do not."

"Oops, wrong answer," John whispered to his team.

"Okay, Todd, you're only small. I will take it easy. I will put my hands behind my back. Okay, now, can you protect yourself from an armless man?" Brown teased again and got more laughter. Jason noticed Giles was laughing too.

Todd nodded and went into a classic karate pose. Brown lunged fast at Todd and stopped just short. Todd stepped back, bringing his arm down to protect an expected blow, but it never came. Brown stood on one leg and kicked out with the other, striking Todd on the face and knocking him back through the ropes.

Jason started to get up but sat back down again. He was angry, but he remembered Wong Tong had told him never to fight in anger. Todd made his way back to his group amid snickers from the older cadets. He sat back down next to Jason and held his nose to stop the bleeding.

Brown spoke again about combat fighting and showed how to break a man's neck, stab someone, and strangle a man. After about an hour, he came to a close.

"Okay, unless we have any more volunteers, that's it," Brown said, folding his arms. Jason looked at Todd, whose face was badly bruised, his confidence shattered.

"Just a minute, Brown," Giles called out. "I am sure we have another karate or kung fu expert here. Would that person like to show us his stuff?"

The cadets glanced around, puzzled. Jason sat still. He could feel Captain Giles eyes burning into him.

"Okay, I'll put it another way. If anyone can put Brown on his back, his team will get ten points."

A few others followed the captain's eyes and looked in Jason's direction, but Jason sat firm. He was not going to fall into the trap. He looked to the floor.

"Maybe I'm wrong. It could be a case of mistaken identity or maybe the cadet is yellow…and all the crap his father says about his spoiled son is just hot air. But I thought we had another cadet who could show us his karate skills."

"Come on, ten points if anyone can put me on my back," Brown said.

Jason knew it was only a matter of time before his name was called by Giles. He might as well turn it into an advantage. After he took a deep breath, he tugged John's shirt.

"What?" John whispered.

"Tell them you will send your youngest and smallest team member into the ring if they double it to twenty points."

"Are you crazy? We already have Todd out now. Look at the state of him. I don't want you to end up like that," John hissed.

"Do you trust me?" Jason asked.

"Are you the guy the captain's asking for?"

"Just do it," Jason said.

John raised his hand.

"Oh, we have a volunteer. Well, come up and see if you can get ten points," Brown said.

John stood up and said, "Sir, if I send my youngest and smallest team member in and he puts you on your back, will you double it to twenty points?"

Several cadets chuckled.

"Double it? I will triple it. Thirty points," Brown said.

John sat back down, and Jason rose to his feet.

"Don't sneeze, Brown. You'll blow him off the ship," shouted a sailor.

Some of the laughter stopped when Jason bent down and started taking his shoes and socks off. He was concerned about his temper. He was furious with Brown for what he had said about karate and what he had done to Todd. The remarks from Captain Giles had only made it worse. He concentrated and tried to calm himself down.

"So, what's your name, cadet?" Brown asked.

"Steed, sir. Jason Steed."

"What can you do, Steed? Karate? Judo? Or just ballroom dancing? What is it?"

Jason ignored him and climbed into the ring.

"Hey, kid, come on. Talk to me. What can you do?"

Again, Jason ignored him and started heavy breathing to fill his blood with oxygen.

"Are you deaf? Is it karate or judo, and what belt are you? It must be something. You have taken your shoes and socks off," Brown said.

"I did not come in here to talk," Jason said calmly.

Brown's smile faded. "Okay, kid, no talking. Come on. Put me on my back."

Jason sprung to his toes and rocked from side to side at an angle to Brown. He didn't move forward. He simply waited.

Eventually, Brown attacked him. He ran and stopped short just as he'd done to Todd. Jason never flinched. He kept rocking gently from side to side on his toes. Brown stepped back and then kicked. Jason dove to the floor, landing on his hands in a pushup position, and swung his legs around, sweeping Brown's leg away from him. Brown's feet flew into the air, and he landed with a heavy thud on his back.

Jason was already standing. He dove down onto Brown, landing his knee on Brown's chest. Jason pulled his right arm back. His clenched fist struck out at Brown's face, stopping less than an inch away from his nose.

"Keeah!" Jason shouted.

The silenced, stunned cadets and crew alike stared wide-eyed at Jason. His fist trembled in anger. He climbed off his opponent and stood up.

"Is karate just for sissies now?" Jason shouted at the top of his voice, looking down at Brown. Shaking, he walked to the side of the ring and picked up his shoes and socks. He looked up at Captain Giles. "That's thirty points for team nine, sir!"

As he climbed out of the ring, he was applauded. Giles turned away, his face void of expression. Slowly, Brown got to his feet, scratching his head.

"Dismissed!" Giles cried.

=

Jason's head was still in a dark cloud as he followed the others down to his bunk room. To his surprise, Sergeant Brown was waiting there, sitting on his bunk. The officer stood up and looked down at them. Todd stepped back in fear.

"You certainly made me look foolish, didn't you, Steed?"

"No, sir, you did that yourself," Jason replied, standing in front of Todd.

The other members of the team waited out in the hallway, stunned by Jason's remark.

"Why did you not hit me?" Brown demanded. "At least get me back for what I did to your friend."

"The objective was to learn hand-to-hand combat. I learned a lot from you: how to break a man's neck and more. It was interesting, but it was not necessary for you to kick Todd in the face just to prove you are bigger and better than him. I proved my point. Hitting you would not have put it across anymore. Karate is not for sissies and is certainly not dancing."

"I would have liked it if you hit him, Jason," Todd said, peering from behind Jason.

Brown smiled. "You're all right, Steed. I like you. I am sorry, Todd. Maybe we all learned something today." He shook Jason's hand and left.

The cadets sighed.

"I thought he was going to kill you, Steed," Rob muttered.

Jason collapsed onto his bunk, exhausted. *I thought he was too*, he admitted to himself. While his team planned for the next day, he closed his eyes and fell asleep.

—

The following week went fast. Every day featured different activities. Jason and Todd stuck together every minute. They ate, slept, swam, and did karate together in their free time. Todd had two sisters, both older than him. He was the baby of the family, and it was the first time he had ever been away from his mother. He spoke of his mother every day. Jason listened, but he couldn't help thinking to himself, *Todd isn't going to last.*

Team nine was still top and was now unreachable by any of the other nineteen teams.

On Friday, they noticed a large ship on the horizon. They found out later that it was the HMS *Ark Royal*. Jason watched it with binoculars.

"That's your father's ship, isn't it, Jase?" Todd asked.

"I haven't been this close to my dad in eight months."

"I don't know how you do it. You must really miss him."

"I don't really know anything different."

═══

The following morning, the cadet teams were given inflatable, motor-ized rafts. The objective was to catch fish if possible and to experience a hot day at sea, fending for their lives. They had to use their water bottles sparingly. Fuel was rationed to a minimum, and they were ordered to keep within a mile of the *Stoke*. Jakarta was two miles to the north. Getting within a mile of the shoreline was strictly off limits.

The fishing was slow. They had no rods, just lines, hooks, and weights. Bait was bread. However, Rob kept some bacon from breakfast. A small breeze slowly pushed the boats north. Every hour or so, they had to start up the tiny motor and move closer to the *Stoke* and farther away from Jakarta.

"We better move back a bit. We are getting too far away," Jeff told John.

"Wait, I have a bite," Rob shouted. The line in his hand was tugging back and forth. He and Jim pulled the line in as fast as they could. They could see the fish in the crystal-clear water just below the inflatable.

"We got one!" Jim screamed. Together, they pulled a large four-pound bass out of the sea.

"Jesus, look at the spikes in its dorsal fin. Watch your hands," John shouted.

The large fish bounced around on the deck of the inflatable, gasping for air.

"Have we got to eat that?" Todd asked, grimacing.

"It's a bass. They are really nice. You'll like it," Rob said.

They could hear the sound of some of the other cadets cheering in the distance. They looked up and could see a high-speed inflatable coming in their direction, carrying four people. One was waving back at the cadets.

"Who's that?" Jim asked.

"I don't know, but look how far we have drifted. Come on, we better start the motor and get back with the rest," John said.

"It's the marines. They must have come from the *Ark Royal*. Look, they are carrying guns," Rob said as it came closer.

They sat and watched as the inflatable bounced across the top of the water at high speed. Todd started waving at them and then Jason followed suit. One of the marines gave a thumbs-up as their inflatable came level.

"It's going to Jakarta," Jeff said. They watched it pass them. The wake made their little inflatable rock from side to side. It was still drifting closer to the shore.

"Look. Choppers," Jeff said.

Three gray-colored helicopters flew low toward them and then they dove. Suddenly, the air was filled with rounds of exploding gunfire. The marines jumped into the sea and dived under the water. The choppers passed over the stunned team nine's inflatable toward the other cadets.

"Is this a training exercise?" Todd gasped.

In a horrifying answer, one of the helicopters opened fire on one of the inflatables carrying cadets. Screams filled the air. The second and third helicopters joined the attack. Some cadets scrambled into the water. Some froze and stared. John pulled the motor cord and started the engine, steering the inflatable back to the *Stoke*. His hands shook violently.

"No," Jason said as calmly as he could muster. "We will be going straight into the helicopters." His eyes darted, trying to make sense of the chaos around him. "Look! The marines are in the water. Their inflatable is sinking."

"We can't help them, Jase. Look at the others. We should help them," John replied, pointing at a group of screaming cadets.

Even from far away, Jason could see they'd been hit. He grabbed the motor handle from John's hand and turned the small raft back toward the marines. The helicopters opened fire over and over again on the tiny boats. Some of the cadets tried to help others. Some were clearly floating lifeless on the surface. As Jason approached the marines, he noticed one was facedown.

"Kids, you gotta get out of here!" a marine treading the red-tinted water shouted.

None answered. They were in a state of shock. Jason stopped the tiny vessel.

"Come on, boys, just keep your heads down and try to get back to the *Stoke*. We can swim from here."

"Sir, they can't go back into that," another marine said. "Move over, boys. We are coming in."

The three large dripping soldiers climbed into team nine's inflatable, nearly sinking it. It would not take much more to submerge the tiny vessel. It was clearly overloaded. "Take it to the shore. We can't take Kevin," the marine told Jason.

"The *Ark* will launch choppers and fighter jets," the first marine announced. He stood over six feet and had a huge chest and biceps. His wet muscular arms shone in the sunlight as he checked his rifle. "They will soon eliminate the choppers and rescue your friends. God, this raft is bloody slow. I'm Major Wilson. This is Peter Tucker and Ryan Lentz. That, in the water, was Kevin Walker. Those choppers are Jakarta rebels funded by the Chinese government."

"Sir, the choppers," Jason said. Two of the helicopters were coming in their direction.

"Keep going," Wilson told Jason while he took aim with his automatic rifle.

As the first helicopter came closer, the marines opened fire. The deafening sound of the high-powered weapons and smell of gunpowder made Jason wince, but he focused on the engine. Todd closed his eyes and grabbed Jason's arm for comfort. The helicopter returned fire. A long stream of bullets rushed across the surface of the sea toward the inflatable. No signal was given by anyone, but they all jumped at the same time. Jason pulled Todd with him into the water.

"Dive!" Major Wilson shouted.

They dived down deep under the surface. Jason went down as far as he could. He waited and looked up through the clear but darkening waters. Bullets still pounded. He could not understand why the water was getting so murky at first. As he slowly started to surface, he then realized the reason. It was colored with blood. He came up for a breath of desperately needed air.

Another round of automatic fire splashed toward them from the helicopters. Again, Jason dove deep. His lungs were screaming for oxygen. His high-paced heartbeat burned his body's limited oxygen supply. Bullets still pounded the surface above. It was a never-ending nightmare. He kept himself under the water as long as he could. His body instinctively took over. He had to surface—and fast.

As Jason gasped for air, he looked for his teammates. The helicopters roared just above him, but at least the shooting had stopped. To his relief, they started to fly back toward the island. He found a body facedown in the water. He turned it over and saw that it was Jim. His head had a large black hole burned into it. It was the first dead body Jason had ever encountered up close. It was the first time someone he'd known had been killed.

"Jason!" Todd coughed and splashed behind him.

He had swallowed a lot of water but was still alive and unhurt. They swam to each other and glanced around.

"Boys, you hurt?" Major Wilson asked.

"We are fine, sir, but, Jim…he's dead," Jason gasped.

"So is this one," Major Wilson said, turning Rob over onto his back. "Okay, boys, can you all stay afloat for a while? It won't be long, and you will be rescued."

"Jason, Todd, over here!" John shouted, clutching Jeff, who was pale and moaning. The water around them was purplish. "Major, Jeff has been hit in the shoulder. Jason, how is Todd?"

"He's swallowed a lot of water, but we will be okay—"

Jeff gave out a terrifying scream. His arms waved and pounded the surface as he fought to keep his head above water. It then became obvious what the problem was. A large gray dorsal fin from a great white shark had broken the water's surface. Jeff disappeared under the deep red water, and another dorsal fin appeared. Jason pulled Todd and started swimming to the shore. He wasn't going to wait in the water and get taken like Jeff. Todd was still having trouble breathing. He was unable to swim in his condition. Jason swam on his back with Todd's head on his chest. Major Wilson took out his revolver and shot at the shark.

"Sir, we've got to get out of here," Ryan shouted.

"Right. Those two boys have the right idea. Let's go," the major ordered. It was at least half a mile away, but remaining would mean certain death.

═

Aircraft carrier HMS *Ark Royal's* Captain Christopher Stephens was on the ship's bridge with Lieutenant Commander Raymond Steed and three other officers when the terrifying radio message crackled through.

"This is the HMS *Stoke*. Captain William Giles. I request immediate assistance. We are under fire. Repeat. We are under hostile attack."

The officers, including Ray Steed, looked through binoculars. They could see the *Stoke* but no attack. The admiralty in London was contacted by Captain Giles. They in turn also contacted the *Ark Royal*.

The communications officer read out the orders.

"Sir, it's true. The *Stoke* has just been attacked by three unidentified combat helicopters."

"Prepare to send two jets immediately," Captain Stephens ordered.

"This is HMS *Ark Royal*. Captain Stephens speaking—we are scrambling two fighter jets. Please confirm your status."

"This is Captain Giles. We have twenty inflatable rafts in the

131

water with British Sea Cadets onboard. They and the marine vessel you launched have been attacked by three combat helicopters. We need as much help and manpower as you can spare. We have one hundred and twenty cadets in the water. We have major casualties. I repeat…major casualties."

Ray Steed ordered twelve rescue launches and four helicopters. Captain Stephens gave orders that any casualties or fatalities were to be brought to the *Ark Royal*, for it had far better facilities than the *Stoke*.

=

In London, it was seven o'clock in the morning. The defense minister was briefed. He drove to Downing Street to inform the prime minister. Exact numbers of fatalities and injuries had not yet been discovered.

=

Ray ran back up to the bridge. Sweat bathed his pale face. The first helicopter at the scene reported a chilling message.

"This is K312. We are above the survivors. We have major fatalities and major injuries."

"This is Captain Stephens. Can you give an estimate?"

"Sir, the sea is red. Bodies are everywhere. As a very rough estimate, I can see at least twenty, maybe thirty—"

"Sir, I need to go and help," Ray requested.

"No, Steed, I need you here." Captain Stephens looked at Ray's face and could see the panic written across it. He called Steed over to the corner of the bridge to speak to him alone.

"Steed, I have known you a long time. It's not like you to panic. Pull yourself together, man."

"Jason is with them. He is a cadet, sir."

"Is that your son?"

"Yes, sir."

"His best chance now is if you do everything here you can. We will find him. For now, I need your full support."

In the background, Ray could hear the sound of gunfire over the radio. The helicopters were trying to shoot some of the sharks that were having a feeding frenzy on the injured and dead cadets.

═══

Major Wilson, Ryan, Pete, and John finally made the shoreline of Jakarta. Jason and Todd were now well behind them, but fifteen minutes after the others had reached safety, Jason's toes scraped the ground. He seized Todd and dragged him to the beautiful, white sandy beach. It stretched far into the distance, ending in a dense tropical plantation of coconut palms and a mass of green shrubbery.

The moment the two boys reached the shore, they came under fire from somewhere in the undergrowth to their left. The marines instinctively opened fire. Ryan took a bullet in his shoulder, but he switched hands and carried on shooting regardless. John, Jason, and Todd buried their faces in the hot sand.

The shooting ceased.

"Come, we need cover!" Major Wilson barked. They stood and ran toward the undergrowth. John stuck close behind Wilson's huge frame. Todd, still coughing, struggled, but Jason pulled Todd's arms over his shoulder and ran with him. The shooting started again. Jason heard a loud thud and found himself tumbling down into the sand. Todd screamed out in pain. Again, the marines returned fire.

Jason rolled Todd over. He coughed a mouthful of blood into Jason's face. His eyes rolled around in his head, and his body squirmed in pain. Jason pulled open Todd's shirt and found that his friend had a huge hole in his chest. Blood bubbled out as he fought to breathe.

"I want to go home," Todd gasped.

"Try not to speak. You're gonna be okay, Todd," Jason said, using his cap to try to stop the bleeding that was frothing from his chest wound.

The shooting ceased. Major Wilson shouted to Jason.

"Kid, drag him here. You're in the open."

Jason got up and lifted Todd up by the shoulders and dragged him up the beach. Again, shots rang out, shooting sand up around Jason, blinding him. Jason kept pulling his friend backward. He ran back as fast as he could among the storm of whizzing bullets. The marines fired back, trying to give him cover.

Two loud thuds came again and ripped Todd's body away from his grasp. Jason jumped to the ground and crawled back to Todd. Again, he rolled him over. Todd had been hit twice in his hip and the side of his body. His body was swimming in blood. Todd grabbed Jason's wrist tightly and stared at him, pleading for help with his eyes. The air bubbles from his chest wound ceased, and his grip on Jason's wrist relaxed and then released. Jason watched Todd's eyes slowly turn lifeless. Jason placed his ear to his friend's mouth to listen for breathing. He tried to find a pulse.

"Todd, come on, talk to me, mate," Jason pleaded. Pete crawled back and joined them. He placed his fingers next to Todd's windpipe for a sign of life.

"He's gone, kid. Get up to the others."

"What about Todd?"

"You did everything you could. Now move!" Pete ordered.

They ran back up to join the group. John was helping Ryan wrap a bandage around his shoulder. Jason was covered in blood and sand.

"You hit, kid?" Wilson asked bluntly.

Jason shook his head, too shocked to speak.

"Let's go. We can't stay here," Wilson ordered.

John carried Ryan's backpack. Jason quietly followed behind as his head spun. It all felt like a bad dream. His friend had died in front of him. Wilson ran through the undergrowth. Jason fought to keep pace and tried wiping the sand from his eyes, but the more he tried, the worse he made it. His hands and arms were covered in sticky blood. He knew he couldn't think. He only knew he had to keep moving.

Chapter Twelve

At nightfall, Wilson ordered the ragtag group of survivors to settle down by a river.

"Do we complete the mission, sir?" Pete asked.

"Yes, it's too important. Ryan, can you carry on?"

"Yes, sir," Ryan grunted. "The bullet went right through."

"What's your name, cadet?" Wilson asked John. "How old are you?"

"John Leigh, sir. I'm nearly sixteen."

"We will need your help. Can you shoot?"

"Yes, sir."

Wilson nodded. "What I am about to tell you is classified, but you need to know the importance of it." He took a deep breath. "Australia and Great Britain joined forces to produce a new type of nuclear weapon. It's far more sophisticated than anything previously produced. Right now, it is aimed at Moscow as part of our joint defense system. That's the good news."

Jason swallowed. His throat was so parched that it hurt. "What's the bad news, sir?" he croaked.

"The technology is advanced and tamper proof. Once set, no one can touch it. Even if your country is destroyed, this baby is still going to go off and bite you back. It's the ultimate in defense. However, the program is on a small cassette, which has been stolen. Intelligence believes by the Chinese. They want nothing more than the Russians and the Western world to fight it out. The Chinese could not admit they are involved, so they traded with the Jakarta government. It's here on the island. If we don't get that cassette back in five days, the missile will launch."

Jason blinked, struggling to process the words.

"Bloody hell," John hissed. "If it is so important, why did they just send you four and not the whole army?"

"They won't give us the whereabouts. We have to meet a man who wants to move his family to the United Kingdom. However, with Kevin dead, that's going to be hard."

"Did Kevin know him?" John asked.

"No, but he spoke Cantonese. Without him, it will be bloody hard, but we have to try. I work better with a team of four. You could be handy, John."

"Sir, you forgot something," Ryan said, pointing with his head and eyes at Jason. He was sitting with his back to them with his head down, desperately trying to keep the insects away that were buzzing around him.

"Kid," Wilson barked. "It's the blood they're after. Go into the river and wash it off. Get it out of your hair and clothes. They'll leave you alone then."

Jason crept down to the river and submerged himself in the cool water. He washed his hair, hands, and as much of his shirt as he could. It cleared his head. He knew he had to pull himself together and stop mourning. Todd was gone, and there was nothing he could do now.

Whereas Ryan was squat and sparse with his words, Peter was tall and lanky—and he was from Newcastle, so every other word he spoke was a swear word. His arms and neck were covered in tattoos. He looked like someone you wouldn't want to get on the wrong side of. Jason could hear him talking. "That bloody kid will slow us down."

"He's not slowed us down yet," Wilson replied. "He helped his friend swim half a mile to shore and practically carried him up the beach. Even under fire, he didn't run. He's got guts, but we can't take him with us. He'll be a liability."

"We can't leave him here. What if he gets captured? He could give out our position and objective," Ryan said.

Jason returned to the others. He looked at his hands. His fingernails were black with dried blood. "Can I borrow your knife please, Ryan?" he asked.

Ryan passed it to him. "Are you going to kill yourself?"

Jason ignored the question and used the point of the blade to clean his nails. He was not sure what to say to Wilson. He asked himself, *What would Scott say?* He tried to think of something. Finally, he took a deep, shaky breath.

"Major, you have three options. One is you leave me here to fend for myself. Chances are the rebels will catch me. If they don't kill me, they may torture me and find out where you are going. I am eleven. I have the same pain threshold of someone my age. Option two is you will have to slit my throat." Jason dropped the knife, and it stuck in the ground at the major's feet. He continued, "When you get back to the *Ark Royal*, you can inform Lieutenant Commander Steed that you slit his only son's throat. He won't be too pleased. Option three is you need someone to speak Cantonese. I grew up in Hong Kong and speak the language. I have not slowed you down and can keep up. I prefer option three, sir."

Wilson cracked a tired smile. "You got guts, kid. How do you know I won't just slit your throat?"

"With Kevin dead, you need me," Jason replied, his fingers crossed.

"Get some sleep. We leave in an hour," the major ordered. He was abrupt but to the point. It was an advantage to keep Jason with them—for now.

═

On the *Ark Royal*, Ray was passed a list of the dead, and he passed it directly to Captain Stephens. The captain's eyes widened, and he shook his head. He sat down and picked up the radio microphone to report to the admiralty.

"This is Captain Stephens from HMS *Ark Royal*. I have a list of the dead and wounded."

═

Back in London, Scott shouted to his parents to come and listen to his ham radio.

"We have sixty-seven dead. I repeat—sixty-seven dead. I will read the names in no particular order." Scott looked at his parents wide-eyed and mouthed "sixty-seven" in astonishment. Scott's parents sat on his bed, holding hands, while he sat at his desk listening with his eyes closed to the broadcast. It took just five minutes to read the sixty-seven names, but it seemed to go on for an eternity.

"We have two critically injured. They have a fifty-fifty chance of survival," the announcer said and read the names of the injured.

Scott looked at his parents. He punched the air with a big smile on his face. However, the captain went on, "Also, four cadets are missing: John Leigh, age fifteen; Todd Johnson, age eleven; Jason Steed, age eleven; Graham Bell, age thirteen. We know one is dead, as we have found another body. Sadly, it is decapitated. We are unable to identify this body."

Scott stood up and shouted at his radio. "No way. Jason is not missing. He can swim like a fish. He can! I've seen him. What the bloody hell are they shooting at him for anyway?"

His mother ran over and hugged him.

"Scott, he is missing. He is not dead," his father said, but it was clear that even he didn't believe his own words.

═══

Her Majesty the Queen held the tea strainer while she poured herself a hot cup of Earl Grey into her bone china teacup. She dropped in a sugar lump, annoyed as it splashed hot tea over her finger.

Catherine watched with the queen and duke as the BBC newscaster read out the names and ages of the boys who had been killed. She held her breath and gasped a sigh of relief—that was, until the names of the four missing boys were called out.

"What are you doing sending them to a war zone?" she cried at her parents. "What is wrong with you? Jason could be dead or hurt somewhere. Daddy, do something." Her voice broke as her body started shaking with sobs.

"I will call the admiralty and see if I can find out something," the duke said. "Your friend is a tough little guy. I am sure he'll make it."

═

Ray Steed traveled by helicopter to the *Stoke*. He was lowered down onto the deck and greeted by his old friend, Captain Giles. "Can I see Jason's bunk room?"

Giles nodded, stood aside, and gestured with his hand. "If you need anything, Ray, just ask."

Ray climbed the stairs down to the bunk rooms. Each room had a card above the open doorway with the team number. When he arrived at team nine's room, he was surprised to see someone going through the clothing in the cabinet. Steed coughed to make his entrance heard. It was Sergeant Brown, who turned and saluted.

"At ease," Ray informed him.

Brown looked at his uniform and read his name badge. "Sir, are you related to Jason Steed?" Brown asked, pointing at his bunk.

Ray nodded and sat down on his son's neatly folded sheets and clothing. "He was my son," he said quietly.

"Sir, he's not dead. I know who the unidentified body is."

"How?" Ray asked and looked up. His bloodshot eyes stared at Brown, looking for any glimmer of hope.

"The body—you know, the decapitated unknown body—is that of a youth, maybe thirteen or fourteen. I am sure of it. John Leigh was almost sixteen. They are all from the same team. I think they swam to shore. The unidentified body is Graham Bell. The shoe size matches Bell's. I have just checked John Leigh's and the karate kids' shoe sizes. No match. It's got to be Bell."

"The karate kids?" Ray asked, puzzled.

"It was our nickname for them. They practiced together in their spare time on deck. Jason is a star on the ship. He kicked my butt big time when I was instructing hand-to-hand combat."

Ray smiled proudly, his eyes filled with tears. He buried his face in his hands and then drew in a breath. His eyes fell on a letter Jason had received from Princess Catherine. He neatly folded it and put it in his pocket. "You think they swam to shore?"

"Yes, sir, it's just a guess, but we have the bodies of Jeff, Rob, and Jim—or what's left of them. I think they swam for it."

Ray stood and nodded. "I must return to the *Ark*. Thank you for what you have done."

"You've got a good kid, sir," Brown replied. "He'll be all right."

Chapter Thirteen

RAY RETURNED TO THE *Ark* and reported to Captain Stephens. "Against orders of the admiralty, I sent a small unit to search the beach," Stephens informed him. "They are coming back, and they have found a body of a very young cadet. I'm sorry, Steed. It doesn't look good for your son."

With a shaky nod, Ray went down to the deck and waited for the small craft to return. Marines wearing black clothing and camouflage-painted faces carried in the covered body of a cadet. They laid the body on the cold metal floor.

"He has been shot, sir. Two, maybe three times. But we believe he was shot on the beach," the first marine told Steed. "The crabs and gulls made lunch of him too. It's not pretty, sir."

Ray bent down. With his hand trembling, he lifted the sheet. He took a deep breath. The body's head was missing. He searched the blood-covered pockets and fumbled across a folded piece of paper—a letter. Some of the words blurred, but it clearly read at the bottom: "Be good, Todd. Love, Mum XX." He felt a flash of relief, and he felt sick for it.

He hurried back to the officers' workroom, where he and Captain Stephens were given brief details of the mission led by Major Wilson. Commander Cunningham from the Royal Marines took control of the meeting.

"So far, it has been a success. We believe that Wilson and two of his platoon are ashore. Kevin Walker was killed. They are now without a translator and fourth man. We expect he may have a cadet with him, John Leigh. Leigh took his inflatable back to pick up the marines. Knowing Wilson, he will use him as a watchout—someone to back them."

Cunningham was interrupted by Captain Stephens.

"How can you say it was a success? We have sixty-eight known dead, two missing cadets, and two others in intensive. Was this a smokescreen? Using Sea Cadets in inflatables so Wilson's crew could go unnoticed through them?"

"The mission on hand is far more important than the Sea Cadets, unfortunately. If we fail to get the cassette back, millions of people will lose their lives. We saw an opportunity and took it. If Wilson can meet with our man on the island and somehow communicate in Cantonese, we have a good chance of recovering the cassette."

"Wilson has a translator," Ray said, hope welling inside him. "We know Todd Johnson made it to shore before he was killed. We suspect John Leigh did. The other missing team member is Jason Steed, my son. He can speak Cantonese. He grew up in Hong Kong. He would have let Wilson know this."

"Lieutenant, you can't really believe Wilson would take an eleven-year-old with him?" Cunningham asked.

"What would you do?" Ray bluntly replied.

—

Wilson, Pete, John, and Ryan hiked as fast as they could through the thick jungle brush. Jason had to jog to keep up.

146

"He said he's going to recommend you get a medal," John whispered to him.

"What? Who did?" Jason asked.

"The Major. For what you did for Todd."

"Well, I didn't do enough. He's dead. No medal will take him home to his mother."

"You can't blame yourself, Jase. You said your father's on the *Ark*. Is that right?" John said.

"We have to keep quiet," Jason whispered. He was in no mood to talk. He was hurt, exhausted, and his friend was dead. And if they didn't succeed in their mission, countless others would be dead soon as well.

Wilson stopped abruptly and removed his binoculars. After a quick peek through them, he spoke quietly to Ryan and Peter and then waved John and Jason forward. "It will be light soon. We need to get under cover and hide out."

After they hiked over a small incline, they found a small valley dense in trees and shrubbery. Pete crawled under a large bush, and the others followed. It was cramped but very well hidden.

"Okay, guys, we need to get some sleep. It will be hot soon, but this should keep us cool," Wilson said, trying to get comfortable amidst the mud and leaves.

Jason lay back and closed his eyes. He discovered he was thirsty and hungry. All he could see was Todd's eyes looking at him as he died. He tried to think of other things: Catherine, Scott, the ship. How many of the cadets had been hurt or killed?

The sun was up when Jason awoke to the sound of Ryan's moaning. The pain in his shoulder had worsened. Peter tried to comfort him by talking lightly spoke about football and what they wanted to do when they got back to England.

"When I get back, I'm gonna have a few pints and watch Liverpool FC on the TV. Then go home with my girlfriend," Pete said, smirking and sucking on a cigarette. "How about you, sir?"

"See my kids. Take my wife out for a meal. And come home and have some private time together," Wilson said.

"What about you, John?" Ryan asked.

"There is a girl I like at school—" John replied, grinning.

They all looked at Jason.

"A trip to Disneyland? Or go out for an ice cream?" Ryan teased Jason. "Come on, kid, if you could be anywhere now, where would you like to be?"

"Back on the *Stoke* with Todd, Jim, Jeff, Rob, and all the others," Jason quietly replied.

His remark stopped the conversation dead for the rest of the day.

=

Once it was dark, Wilson announced his plan. "About seven miles from here is the village. It will take us approximately two hours to get there. We have to cross the river. It's deep and fast. You need to swim fast without splashing—can you do that?"

John and Jason nodded.

"When we get to the other side, kid, you stick with me. John, stay with Ryan and Peter."

As they crept on again, Jason said to himself, *he calls John by his name. Why does he have to call me kid?* But he knew it was just the hunger, thirst, and exhaustion talking. Everything irritated him.

As they approached, they could hear the Angke River. It was over sixty feet deep and a hundred feet across. Wilson waded straight in, and Jason followed. By the time he was waist-deep, the current was already pulling him off track. Wilson started swimming upstream at an angle. Swimming straight across would carry them a mile downstream by the time they reached the other bank. After half an hour, they'd only made it halfway across the river. Jason's body was tired. He was hungry, and he needed sleep. He watched Wilson's shaved head glistening in the moonlight. Wilson kept on going, and Jason continued to follow, wondering where John, Pete, and Ryan were. He didn't dare look back and lose valuable ground. He could no longer swim quietly. His arms and legs were heavy, and they made splashes. With each powerful energy-zapping stroke, his breathing became heavy as he fought for air. He closed his eyes and kept going as fast as he could against the powerful current.

A hand grabbed his collar.

"Can you reach the bottom?"

It was Wilson, who was now standing waist-deep. They were just a few feet from the shore. Jason put his feet down, but they were quickly swept away. He was too short and light to stand. Wilson pulled him back and walked the rest of the way, dragging Jason by his collar.

"It's below my waist now," Jason gasped, staggering ahead. He looked behind but could not see the others in the darkness. He and

Wilson waded out of the water to the bank. Jason knelt down on his hands and knees, trying to get his breath back.

"Kid, you said you wouldn't slow me down—come on." Jason pulled himself to his feet and followed. After maybe twenty minutes, the lights of a village peeked through the trees. Wilson pulled out a small map. Using a cigarette lighter, he looked it over. Jason used the opportunity to sit down.

"Okay, this way," Wilson ordered. He got up again after a three-second rest and carried on walking. They crept along a tiny mud road. Every thirty feet or so was a small home, mostly constructed from mud and tin. Jason's wet boots and socks rubbed his feet. Every step became more painful. He knew there was no point saying anything to the major. He just had to keep following.

Wilson stopped and looked at his map once more.

"This is it, kid," he breathed. "Stay close behind me." They crept up to the entrance of a small home. A large, thick gray cloth hung over the doorway to make a door. Wilson held his rifle at waist level and slowly pulled the cloth back. They tiptoed inside.

Jason was shaking uncontrollably. He tried hard to stop. He was not sure if it was fear, hunger, exhaustion, or a combination of everything. He had not eaten since breakfast the previous day.

"You're on, kid," Wilson whispered as something stirred in the house. First in Malay and then in Cantonese, a frightened voice called, "Who is there?"

"We won't harm you. This is the Royal Marines," Jason replied.

"I am Lee Chu."

Wilson flicked on his cigarette lighter and lit a candle. The yellow flame revealed Lee Chu and his wife, lying on a mattress on the floor. Next to them was another mattress with two small children. All of them stirred and yawned. In the corner were a table and four chairs, some wooden boxes on the floor, and a tiny wood-burning stove. Damp clothing hung across the room. Lee Chu slowly got up and walked toward Jason.

"Let me see it first," Lee Chu said.

Jason turned to Wilson. "He wants to see something. Do we have something for him?"

Wilson was looking out a small gap between the doorway and the cloth door. He pulled a plastic bag from his pocket and threw it in Jason's direction.

Jason walked over to the table and sat down. He invited the man to sit, while he opened the bag and spilled its contents on the table. It contained $5,000 in U.S. currency and a letter granting him and his family refugee status in Great Britain. The letter was written in English and Chinese. It had been signed by the British defense minister himself.

The man read the letter and smiled. "We have it," he told his wife, who then nodded and smiled. The two children had joined her on her bed. They watched Jason's every move with their large black eyes. It was obvious that they had not seen many Westerners. A boy with blond hair must have been very rare. Jason noticed a very large bunch of bananas on the floor.

"I need you to keep your end of the agreement and tell me where the cassette is," Jason said. "Plus I need something else."

Lee Chu angrily barked in English, "I tell you where the cassette is—nothing else."

Jason put his hand on the letter and money and pulled it back toward him. Wilson stepped toward the table and raised his rifle at Lee Chu.

"Is there a problem, kid?"

"No, sir, it's all right. Please leave it to me," Jason turned back to Lee Chu. He pushed the contents back to his side of the table. "Please sit. You're right. That's all you have to give us. I wanted something else. If you say no to the additional request, you still get this."

Lee Chu sat down and nodded. "What else do you want?" he asked in Cantonese.

"I have not eaten in two days. Can I have some fruit please?"

Lee Chu started laughing, exposing brown, decayed teeth. He stood and pulled six bananas from the large bunch and passed them to Jason.

"Thank you. Where is the cassette?" Jason asked, hungrily peeling a banana.

One of the children, a boy aged about three, wearing just his underwear, walked over and stood next to Jason and stared at him while his father spoke and Jason wolfed down the fruit. He couldn't remember anything ever tasting so delicious.

Lee Chu informed Jason that a man named Chung Weing had the cassette. Chung Weing owned most of the land in the area. He lived in a large complex facing the Angke River. It was nearly the size of an airport, and it also included barracks for his private army. Lee Chu added that Weing collected World War II items, such as German Sherman tanks, U.S. jeeps, and many vintage aircraft, including a British Spitfire and a huge U.S. B-24 bomber. The cassette was in Weing's safe, which was guarded twenty-four hours a day. The safe was in the library behind a hidden bookcase. China didn't want the cassette on their soil, so they stashed it here in return for weapons to Weing.

Lee Chu stood and went to a black wooden box covered with damp towels. He opened it and removed a large clay bottle, which he placed on the table. He then placed a small tin cup on the table and pushed it toward Jason, who was already on his sixth banana. Jason opened the jug and poured some of the contents into the cup. Jason took a mouthful and almost spit it out. It was goat's milk and not that fresh. Jason swallowed it anyway and drank the rest with his eyes closed. Wilson glared at Jason but had no idea how the conversation was going. Jason got up and wiped the milk from his lips. He thanked Lee Chu. He looked at the small boy next to him and smiled.

"I'm Huan. What's your name?" the boy asked.

"Hello, Huan. I'm Jason. It's nice meeting you."

Wilson faked a loud cough. Jason looked up at him and said, "Okay, sir, I have everything we need to know."

With a bow to Lee Chu and his wife, Jason followed Wilson out the door. They left the village and crept along the outskirts. Wilson stopped and crouched down. They could hear what sounded like an owl hooting. Wilson hooted back with the same sound. "Pete," he hissed.

"Yes, sir," replied a voice in the darkness. They crawled forward and found Pete, Ryan, and John hiding behind some bushes ten meters from the road.

"Wow, he made it across the river. I very much doubted that. We almost lost John," Pete said, looking at Jason.

"We made contact. The kid has the details and location of the cassette," Wilson said. His stomach growled as he sat down. Jason knew just how hungry he was. He wondered why he hadn't asked for any food himself.

Jason then explained everything Lee Chu had told him regarding Weing and where the cassette was located. Wilson gave the orders to move forward. Jason's feet still hurt, but after his meal of bananas and sour goat's milk, he had gotten some strength back. John patted Jason on the back as they marched into the night.

"I bet you never thought we would be on a real live mission. Isn't it great?" John whispered.

"You think this is fun?" Jason snapped. "Tell that to the rest of our team's parents."

John swallowed. "I'm trying to put a brave face on—that's all."

Jason nodded. "I know. I'm sorry. We'll get out of here."

"I hope so," John said. "If we do, we'll all owe you."

=

Turned out that a dozen or so armed guards patrolled the barbed-wire fence around Weing's compound. Wilson waved for the others to duck down, waiting for the right moment. Jason held his breath as Wilson fixed a silencer on his revolver and slipped it into the front of his belt. After he checked his rifle, he gave the silent order to move, pointing toward the point of entry. He pulled a bandanna from his pocket and handed one to Jason. Pete did the same for John. The moment the guards were out of sight on their patrol route, Wilson and the other two marines ran through the shadows toward the fence. Jason and John scurried after them.

Jason only understood why they'd given him a bandanna when Wilson threw his on top of the barbed wire and clamped down on it, hurtling himself over the fence. Jason did the same. His heart was pounding so loud he was certain the guards would hear him. The team ran for cover behind some oil drums.

Fortunately, the many vehicles threw shadows that hid them from the moonlight as they crept along behind the buildings. Wilson held his hand up to halt his team.

"Pete's coming with me," he whispered. "John and Ryan, you cover us."

Jason was ordered to stay out of sight and remain behind. Ryan passed John his pistol.

"Here, kid," John said, passing Jason his knife.

Jason ducked down behind a pile of wooden planks as the others left him and scurried down the dimly lit road. He heard footsteps from behind—a guard walking in the team's direction. A few more steps, and he would have a full view of them. Maybe Wilson or Ryan would shoot the guard with a silenced revolver, but maybe he would not only shoot them but wake up the whole complex. There was no time to think. It was now or never. Jason climbed over the pile of wood and dived at the guard, sticking his fist in the guard's mouth so he could not call out.

They both fell with a loud thud on the gravel road. Wilson and his team turned at the sound. Jason's victim bit hard on his fist. Without a second thought, Jason pulled out the knife and thrust it at the guard's chest. To his surprise, it didn't go in. The guard had something in his top pocket, and it protected him. Again, Jason brought the knife down, this time catching the guard in his throat.

The knife went in deep, up to the handle. The guard stopped biting Jason's hand. Jason then pulled out his hand and covered the guard's mouth while he twisted the knife, trying to cut through his windpipe. The guard shook violently. Pete started running back to help.

Ryan whispered, "What the hell do they put in kids' cornflakes nowadays?"

Jason stood and lifted the guard by his collar. He started to drag him back behind the pile of wood. Pete and Ryan nodded approval at Jason and went back to join the others.

Jason clutched the knife as he slunk back into his hiding place. His hands were soaking wet. Was it sweat? It was too dark to see. He smelled his hands and quickly learned that it was blood. His stomach churned. He threw up and lost his meal of bananas and goat's milk. Tears welled up in his eyes. He shook his head.

I've killed a man. I've done what I never wanted to do—

Those who studied and took martial arts seriously knew that the true masters were nonviolent—that the beauty lay in discipline—but Jason hadn't had a choice. It was kill or be killed out here—

A shot rang out. Jason bolted upright. The complex lights came on, and a siren sounded. Guards poured out of the building, partly dressed, carrying automatic rifles. Wilson took a bullet in his right shoulder. Pete was the next to fall. A bullet went through his left arm. John dropped his gun and dove to the ground. Ryan was shot in the ankle. The shooting ceased, and there was shouting. The guards surrounded Wilson's team and took the weapons off them. They shouted abuse at Wilson in Cantonese. Some of the words Jason had never heard before.

With that, Jason ran back to the fence and climbed back out of the complex, sprinting until he came to some long grass. He lay down, raising his head enough to peek through. Some of the guards were walking back up the road. They were only visible when they walked past the gaps between the buildings. Then, Jason spotted Wilson, Pete, Ryan, and John, who had their hands raised, surrounded by gunmen.

As they approached the area Jason had been hiding in, one of Weing's guards noticed blood on the gravel road. He followed the trail and found the guard Jason had killed. He shouted to the others, and they began frantically searching the area.

It would soon be dawn. Jason lay there thinking about what he should do next. His body was tired and hungry. He could do nothing until the following night, so he decided to find a place to sleep.

He ran through the undergrowth, keeping parallel with the complex. He passed the buildings and Weing's home. On a runway, he could see Weing's collection of World War II toys: tanks, the Spitfire, and a B-24 U.S. bomber at the very end of the runway.

As quietly as he could, Jason made his way to the B-24, opened the heavy door, and climbed in through a hatch on its massive underside. He crawled up beneath on of its three Plexiglas domes, which reminded him of fishbowls. One was at the top of the plane, one at the tail, and one at the belly. All were armed with twin high-powered machine guns.

Jason found his way to the cockpit and sat in the pilot's seat. The plane was fueled and ready to go. He had never flown a real plane and had never flown anything as big or old as this in a simulator, but the controls looked similar. As he tried to figure out what he was going to do, he fell asleep.

Chapter Fourteen

WEING HAD PICTURES TAKEN of Major Wilson, Pete, Ryan, and John. That morning, he slipped them to the press and accused Great Britain of spying on Jakarta. The British government denied it, and the official word was that they were part of the rescue mission and had been captured by Weing's rebels.

=

Back in London, the duke was given an update. He had to break the news to Catherine. John Leigh, one of the missing cadets, was being held prisoner. Only Jason was missing. He told her to be brave and expect the worst. Jason had probably been killed in the sea. Catherine had not eaten in two days. She was so depressed that they fetched a doctor to see her.

=

Scott now realized that he might have to accept that his friend was dead. He constantly monitored the radio for news, but none came—only more reports of waiting and waiting.

=

Mr. and Mrs. Macintosh attended their local church in Scotland and prayed for Jason. It had been hard enough for them to lose their only daughter. The only comfort they had was that she had given birth to Jason. The local people in the small Scottish village came by to offer help and support.

═══

Jason was awakened by stifling heat.

The B-24 was dark green and absorbed the sunlight. Plus, the dawn's rays seeped through the cockpit and Plexiglas domes. He had no idea what time it was, but the sun began to set fairly soon after he woke up. He desperately tried to come up with a plan. He was thirsty and hungry. Every few minutes, he found himself picturing cold milkshakes, glasses of iced fruit juice, and water flowing from faucets in sparkling streams.

Darkness fell, and he still hadn't thought of a single thing other than food and drink. In frustration, he stood and kicked at the floor, and his foot connected with a thick coil of rope. Suddenly, his plan clicked into place.

As he seized the rope, he climbed out of the plane and dashed to the river, where he found a broken tree stump at the bank. After he had gotten undressed, he climbed into the water and tied one end of the rope around the tree stump. As he held the other end, he allowed the current to take him downstream. Once level with the house, he dived to the bottom. While there, he searched for large rocks, tying the rope to the biggest of the lot. After he pulled himself back upstream, he surfaced, out of breath, back at the tree stump.

As he climbed out, he noticed some duck eggs in a nest.

Without a second thought, he cracked them and drank them raw. They didn't taste that bad. Besides, he knew eggs were a good source of protein and energy, something he badly needed. He got dressed as fast as he could, his body soaked, as mosquitoes swarmed to dine on him. He then used mud from the river bank to darken his face and hair. He lay flat on his front and used his elbows and knees to inch his way to Weing's home. Two guards stood outside. Jason crawled painfully slow to the back of the house.

His ears, face, and wrists had already been bitten raw. He watched helplessly as insects landed on him and stung. They buzzed around his ears. A guard stopped and looked in Jason's direction and lit a cigarette before he moved off.

Jason wasn't sure how long it had taken him to reach the house undetected. An hour? Two? Or just minutes? He tried several windows, but they were all locked. Finally, he came across a small mesh window—just under a foot square, too small for an adult to get through but perfect for Jason. With his knife, he slowly cut through the mesh. Every few moments, he stopped and listened. The night was still and quiet except for the buzzing of insects. He cut through three sides, bent the mesh back, and then squeezed headfirst into the dark hole.

Once he was inside, he realized that he was in the food pantry. The kitchen light was on, its glow filtered under the door. He felt around for some food and came across a tin of corn beef, which he stuffed into his pocket for later. He held his ear to the inside of the pantry door, trying to hear any movement.

As he held his breath, he slowly opened the door. The bright fluorescent lights blinded him for a few moments. He crept into the kitchen and looked around. Luckily, it was empty. Half of a glass of Coke was on the table. Jason picked it up to drink it but stopped short when he smelled it. There was whiskey in the soda. He then found the open can and ravenously drank from it.

Re-energized, he tiptoed into a passageway. Above him loomed a massive stairwell. The home was very lavish. Everywhere he looked he saw tapestries and huge statues of ferocious animals. The floor was covered in wall-to-wall white carpet, which helped muffle his steps. As he crept farther into the hallway, he could hear music and laughter coming from a room to his left.

The door was slightly ajar, allowing him to peek through the crack. Inside was a fat little man sitting on a couch with two young Chinese girls, who did not look more than fifteen years old. They were rubbing his blubbery chest. Jason backed up and walked to the other room. The door was wide open, but the lights were turned off. The room was lined with bookshelves. That's when Jason remembered that Lee Chu had told him the cassette was hidden in a safe in the library.

After he searched the books for a trigger that would open a secret closet for ten minutes, he gave up and tried the mahogany desk. In the drawer, he found a handgun. Because he had never used a gun before, he checked first to see if it was loaded and also if it had a safety catch. It did, but it was already turned off.

Slowly, he walked out of the library and took a deep breath. He tried to stop his hands from shaking and marched straight into the living room, where Weing was being entertained.

All three of their jaws dropped at once.

In Chinese, Jason spoke firmly to Weing and the two girls. "If you make one sound, I will kill you. If you don't do as I say, I will kill you."

The girls shrieked and threw up their hands.

"Boy, do you know who I am? I am Weing! How dare you come into my home!" the little man barked. He leapt to his feet, grunting at his own weight.

Jason twisted on one foot and side-kicked Weing direct in the face, sending him back on the couch.

"I told you not to make a sound. One more sound and I will kill you."

Weing's beady eyes bulged. His nose was bleeding. Jason looked at the two girls. He was slightly embarrassed by their semi-clothed bodies. "You two, move into the library...slowly. You too, Weing. Now. I'm serious."

They walked past Jason with their hands raised. Jason followed them. Of course, Weing shot Jason an evil glare.

"Open the bookcase," he ordered.

"What bookcase?" Weing snapped.

Jason froze. Had Lee Chu lied to him? He'd trusted him, but all Lee Chu had wanted was to take his family to the UK. It had to be this fat little slob who was lying. Jason pointed the gun at Weing's chest.

"You have five seconds to open it or I'll shoot," Jason said. Sweat poured from his forehead, washing the mud into his eyes. To his relief, Weing walked over to the bookcase and slid it along the wall. Behind it was a steel safe.

"Open it," Jason ordered.

"If I refuse, you will never get what's inside. How do I know you won't kill me anyway?"

"You have a simple choice. Open it and hope I don't kill you… or don't open it and die." Jason swallowed, his mind racing. "My platoon is outside. So, what is it going to be?"

Weing turned and opened the safe. He put his hand in and said, "Is this what you want?"

Jason caught the flash of a revolver as Weing whirled back around to face him. Without thinking, Jason squeezed the trigger. The bullet struck Weing in the head. He immediately collapsed to the floor. Jason winced. The pistol was loud and gave a heavy kickback—something he did not expect. The girls screamed and crouched down on the floor.

That's two people I've killed, he thought sickly.

But there was no time for regrets or second-guessing. Jason ran over to the desk, stepped over Weing's body, looked in the safe, and found a small wooden box. With trembling fingers, he opened it and found a metal cassette tape in a plastic bag. He grabbed it and stuffed it down the front of his underwear. As he did, the front door to Weing's house burst open. Heavy-booted footsteps clattered down the hall.

Jason's eyes darted to the window. He held his breath, squeezed his eyes closed, and hurtled himself into the glass, fists first, rolling to the ground and springing back to his feet. As he started sprinting, he examined his knuckles in the moonlight. They were bleeding, but he didn't seem to have any shards of glass stuck in his flesh. With the pistol still in hand, he dashed toward the river. Voices shouted behind him, and shots rang out.

This was no assault course. This was for real. Bullets landed around his feet, behind him to his left and right. He heard a sound like a firecracker as a bullet skimmed past his ear. Then, he felt a sharp pain in the back of his right leg. Adrenaline kept him from falling, but he limped the last few yards to the river bank. With the sound of machine gun fire now muffled by the incline, he dove deep into the water.

Struggling blindly, holding his breath, his leg stinging, he fought through the current and felt his way along the riverbed until he finally found his rope. His lungs began to burn. He was running out of oxygen. Above him, the muffled sound of gunfire continued to strafe the surface. Panic seeped in and quickened his heart rate. He clenched down hard on his jaw and focused on the rope. No matter how much it hurt and how desperate he needed to breathe, he had to keep going. If he came up for air, it would mean sudden death. He felt light-headed. He exhaled his last breath in a cloud of murky bubbles as he plodded forward against the current. The rope seemed to go on forever, but he finally reached the end and was able to surface behind the tree stump. As he heaved, he collapsed amongst the reeds.

Meanwhile, the guards searched with spotlights downstream. He could hear them chattering in Cantonese. No one could possibly swim upstream. They also found some of Jason's blood on the bank and suspected he may have been killed.

As Jason tried to stand, his right leg gave way. He fell back down in pain. Only now did he realize that the bullet had gone through his hamstring muscle, and his leg was covered in blood. He took off a sock and tied it tightly around his wound to slow the bleeding. Soaking wet and back on his feet, he limped through the reeds to the dark tarmac and finally pulled himself into the B-24.

The silence and stuffy warmth inside was a blessed relief from the gunfire and chaos he'd just escaped.

In the cockpit cabinet, he found a first aid kit. He removed his pants to look at the damage the bullet had done. The entry wound was small, but the exit wound was twice the size. Who would have thought that the course he'd taken on the HMS *Stoke* on "First Aid in the Battlefield" would have come in handy so fast? Jason knew he had to clean the deep gashes, so he applied iodine and alcohol solution. Searing pain shot through him. It took his breath away, and he momentarily lost consciousness. When he came back to his senses, he was on the cold metal floor, panting and groaning. He scowled at the bottle still clenched in his fist.

"Guess they left out the part about how it bloody stings," he spat out loud.

His face bathed in sweat, Jason collapsed into the pilot's seat and scratched his mosquito bites. He knew it wouldn't help, but for a few brief moments, the fingernails felt good on his flaming skin.

After a few deep, measured breaths, he dressed his bullet wound with gauze and tossed the first aid kit into the copilot's seat. Then, he fumbled for the can of fatty corn beef in his wet pocket. After he wolfed it down with his dirty fingers, he felt a little better than before—at least clearheaded enough to turn on the power in the plane and figure out his next move. In the darkness, he reached for the power switch.

With a loud click, the plane buzzed to life.

The control panel lit up. The radio cracked and hissed. Jason's heart began pounding again. He peered out the window, but the tarmac was still deserted. Every second counted. It could be dangerous to transmit a message that could be picked up by Weing's guards or even the Chinese. Slowly, he clicked the dial until it read 36.5. *Would Scott be tuned in?* he wondered. He had no idea what time it was in London. In a flash, however, he made his decision. He clicked the microphone on and off and sent a message by Morse code.

The series of dots and dashes he sent was:

.. / .... .- ...- . / .-- .... .- - / -.-- --- ..- /
.-- .- -. - / .- -. -.. / .-- .. .-.. .-.. /
. -..- -.-. .... .- -. --. . / .. - / ..-. --- .-. /
... --- -- . / -.-. .- .-. .-. --- - /
-.-. .- -.- . .-,-.-

When finished, he repeated the message and then turned off the radio, afraid it could be traced. *Could Scott even decipher Morse code, even if he was listening?* Jason had no idea.

═══

It was 9:00 p.m. in London. Scott was in his room, unable to sleep. He'd slept maybe four hours in the last two days. His radio hadn't once been turned off. He lay on his bed, trying to read when he heard the clicking. At first, he ignored it, but when he recognized that it was a pattern—and that the pattern repeated—he wrote it down. He grabbed a book on radio signals from his shelf and flipped to the section on Morse code.

The words translated: "I have what you want and will exchange it for some carrot cake."

Scott looked at the message over and over again. A smile crept across his face. It had to be…Jason. It had to be. Who else would be jabbering about carrot cake? Eventfully, he shouted at the top of his voice, "*Yes!*" He ran down the stairs into the living room and picked up the telephone directory.

"What's wrong, Scott?" his mother asked.

"How stupid I was. How stupid, stupid, stupid. How could I have doubted him? Jason is alive and kicking." He found a number to the Scotland Yard, Britain's Police HQ.

A secretary answered. Scott breathlessly informed him that Jason Steed, the last of the missing Sea Cadets from the news stories, had just made contact from Jakarta. The man chuckled.

"Thanks, lad. I'll pass the message on."

Click.

Scott frowned at his stunned parents. "They don't believe me. I guess they think I am just a kid, but I know it's Jason."

═══

Less than twenty minutes later, police sirens broke the silence of the quiet London suburb street of Churchwood Avenue. Two police cars screeched to a halt and were followed by a large black Rover 3500. Dr. and Mrs. Turner peered out the front room window. Scott ran to the door just as the pounding began.

"We had a phone call from a Mr. Scott Turner. Is that you, sir?" a tall gray-haired man with a deeply pitted face asked. He was accompanied by three uniformed police officers.

"No, that's my son. Is he in trouble?" the doctor asked, stepping in front of his son.

"For his sake, I hope not. I am Lawrence Cox."

Scott ran to the stairs. "That was fast. Come up, and I will show you what I've heard." The men followed, trailed closely by Scott's parents.

"Can I get anyone a cup of tea?" Mrs. Turner asked anxiously.

"No, thank you. We're fine," Cox replied. He sat on Scott's bed. "You called Scotland Yard and said that Jason Steed had contacted you from Jakarta. How exactly?"

"Morse code, sir. Look, this is what it means." Scott grabbed his notebook from the desk and showed them. His hands were shaking with excitement.

"Yes, we also have that message. What makes you think this is Jason Steed?"

Scott took a framed picture off the wall and passed it to them. "That's me and Jase dressed up in our dinner suits. We went to a Christmas party together. He's my best friend and sleeps here some weekends. No one eats and loves carrot cake like Jason. He has it every day, and he knows I have my ham radio tuned into 36.5 FM."

Cox nodded, his face expressionless. "So, apart from making assumptions, you have no proof?"

Scott's face darkened. He counted off on his fingers. "Unless you know of someone else in the Jakarta region who loves carrot cake, is missing, has something you want, and knows that I listen in on that radio channel…then it's Jason."

"Have you any idea what he has of ours?" Cox asked.

Scott shot a nervous glance at his parents, who stood in the doorway. "Not exactly. All I know is that it's what you are looking for. You sent a bunch of cadets a mile offshore of a war zone for something, and you got most of them killed and my mate in danger—"

"Please, Scott," Dr. Turner interrupted.

Cox shook his head. "No, it's all right. Go on, lad."

"My point is that you know what it is he's got," Scott said. "If not, you would not have come over here so fast."

For a moment, Cox was silent. He shot the policemen an unreadable stare. "Master Turner, you are a very bright young man," he said gravely. "I hope for your friend's sake and our country that you're right. All I can say is that I hope he can get away."

"If anyone can, he can," Scott replied. "I know it."

———

Back onboard the *Ark Royal*, Ray walked wearily into the officers' mess. Captain Stephens sat talking to the special operations crew. They were all exhausted by the last two days' events. Ray had not slept or eaten much either. He had started to give up on the idea of ever seeing Jason again. He collected a plate of food and went and sat alone at a table.

The captain joined him. "How are you managing, Ray?"

"Hour by hour. I can't think ahead. I had been looking forward to my leave in September. I was going to take Jason on a holiday somewhere." His voice grew thick. He swallowed and blinked. "Has there been any news of the prisoners?"

"No, Ray, we are waiting for Downing Street to come up with a negotiation strategy to get them back. We did get a message via

Morse code today. The admiralty has no idea what it means but is following up on a lead."

Ray picked at his meat and vegetables, trying to force some food into his churning stomach. All he could think was: *If Jason is alive and hiding somewhere, does he have any food and water?*

The captain didn't say anything more. Ray was appreciative, but he didn't feel like talking. He was about to leave when a member of the special operations crew burst into the officers' mess and glanced around the room until he spotted Ray.

"Hello, Lieutenant Steed. I am Major John Evans. I have just been contacted from London via the telex. Do you know someone called Scott Turner?"

Ray looked up from his food, puzzled. "Scott Turner? Sure, he's a friend of my son's. Why?"

"Would he know Jason very well?" Evans asked.

"Yes, they go to school together and spend most weekends at my home or Scott's home. He probably knows Jason better than anyone. Why? Is he all right?"

"He has been monitoring our radio waves, and he picked up the same Morse code message we did. He says it's from Jason."

"The carrot cake message?" Captain Stephens asked.

Evans nodded. "Yes, did you not see the message, Steed?"

"No, what did it say? When was this?"

Evans handed Ray a crumpled printout. "This Scott Turner swears it's from Jason."

A warm rush of relief flooded through Ray as he read the note. "It is. When he was a toddler, that's all they could get him to eat. He loves the stuff. He's alive. He has what we want? Jesus Christ, he must have the cassette."

"Then he was with Major Wilson. They never caught him." Captain Stephens said.

Ray leapt to his feet. "Come on, we have to move—"

"Lieutenant Steed," Captain Stephens interrupted. "We can't step foot on the island. He will have to figure a way out unless we can negotiate his release, but the Chinese are still denying any involvement. It may come to sending in a strike force, but we are holding off. The Chinese have a battleship just north of Jakarta. It is expected to be coming this way for observation purposes."

Ray's jaw tightened. "The kid is eleven. What the hell do you want him to do? Steal a boat and sail back to us?"

Evans and Captain Stephens exchanged a glance.

"I can't say I know how you are feeling, Steed, as I don't," Evans replied. "All I know is we now have less than forty-eight hours to get that cassette back. Your son has it, and we have no way of contacting him. I have to report back. I will keep you informed."

Ray turned to Captain Stephens.

"Remarkable, isn't it?" Captain Stephens said gently.

"What is?"

"With all our firepower, money, and technology, our best intelligence came down to two kids thousands of miles apart working it out on a ham radio."

Ray shook his head. "That's not remarkable. What will be remarkable is getting my son back alive."

Before Captain Stephens could respond, Ray coldly saluted and left.

Chapter Fifteen

BACK ON THE B-24, Jason redressed his leg. It was stiff and difficult to move. Even the slightest pressure caused pain, but at least the bleeding had stopped.

The swift sunrise once again heated the cockpit until it felt like a sauna. Jason limped down to the plane's galley, where in the darkness he discovered some water rations and potato crisps. After he gobbled down two bags, he fell into an uneasy slumber.

When he awoke, it was dark again. *Time to move*, he thought. He crept out of the plane and silently limped toward the center of the complex. As he kept clear of the buildings and guards, he eventually came to the end of the road and found the familiar pile of wood where he had hidden. Jason noticed the blood from the guard he had killed was still on the path. A twinge of guilt shot through him, but he shook it off. He had to find Wilson and the others. They were either dead or being held captive. He couldn't leave until he knew their fates for certain.

At the far end of the complex stood a squat stone building with barred windows. *Most likely a prison*, Jason thought. Outside on a wooden box sat a guard smoking a cigarette, a machine gun propped next to him. Jason chewed his lip. Wong Tong had always taught him to use the element of surprise. "Surprise even yourself," he had said. "It's the best weapon you will ever have."

His decision made in an instant, Jason coolly limped up to the guard and spoke in Cantonese, "You want to buy some cigarettes at a very cheap price?"

The guard glared at him and stood.

"How much, and how many?" Jason asked, grinning.

"Who are you?" the guard demanded, reaching for his gun. "How did you get onto—?"

"I am the bogeyman," interrupted Jason. He dove to the ground, and with a slide kick, he swept the shocked guard's feet away from him. He ignored the pain from his gunshot wounds and sprang to his feet and seized the gun, slamming the butt into the guard's forehead. The guard rolled over and lay still, unconscious. Jason glanced at the door. It was open.

The hinges made a slight creak as Jason entered. He cringed, gripping the machine gun tightly. A guard lay sleeping on a torn sofa positioned at the opening of a long narrow corridor lined with doors on either side. Without hesitation, Jason seized the guard by his neck, squeezing it tightly from behind in a Judo sleeper hold. Jason had never used the technique before, but it worked with surprising speed and effectiveness. After the guard kicked his feet, he slumped in Jason's arms, unconscious. Jason found a key ring on his belt and unhooked it.

Each door had a small window at the top with bars. Jason stood on his tiptoes and peered through the first one and saw that it was empty. The next two were also empty. In the fourth, however, a man he didn't recognize lay sprawled on the floor. Alive or dead, Jason couldn't tell. He was starting to lose hope until he reached the fifth room, but there, chained to the wall, were Wilson and his team.

With trembling fingers, he tried key after key until the lock finally clicked. The door swung open. The prisoners watched in shocked silence as the small figure shuffled into their cell. They recognized the uniform he was wearing, although it was blood-stained, dirty, and torn.

"Jason? Is that you?" John gasped.

On the far side of the room, a cracked and filthy mirror hung before the chained prisoners. Perhaps Weing had made them stare at themselves all day as a form of torture, but when Jason caught a glimpse of himself, he knew why John had asked the question. His hair was unwashed. His face was pale, dirty, and cut, covered in mosquito bites and splattered with blood. His pants were ripped open, revealing part of the bloodstained dressing on his dirt-covered leg. His blue eyes had lost their sparkle. They were now dark and sunken.

"Follow me, and don't make a sound," Jason groaned as he unlocked their shackles. "We have a plane to catch."

===

Fifteen minutes later, after a harrowing, zigzagging journey through the compound and a brutal climb over the barbed wire, Jason and the others reached the tarmac. The B-24 loomed at the far end, silhouetted against the moonlight. Jason broke into a limping run, but a strong hand clamped down on his shoulder.

He whirled around.

"Jason," Wilson hissed. "How did you do this? Have you contacted our forces?"

He took a deep breath, sighed, crouched down, and gestured to the others to crouch down in a small group.

He spoke softly, "Sir, I have the cassette. I have not been in contact with anyone. Just follow me. We are going home. Please keep quiet."

"How are we getting out of here?" Ryan demanded.

"We are flying, sir. We have to move. It will be light soon. Can we move on, sir?"

Wilson nodded and stood. "You've gotten us this far, Jason. We'll follow your lead. We owe you our lives."

As Jason stood, his right leg gave way, and he fell to the ground. Pain like he had never felt before shot through his body. He bent forward on his knees and pushed his forehead hard against the ground and twisted his head into the gravel to prevent himself from screaming out loud.

Without saying anything, John bent down and helped him to his feet. Together, they scrambled to the B-24. Jason swung open the metal door in its belly.

"You have got to be kidding, Jason," Pete said.

Jason ignored him and climbed in. They followed and closed the door.

"Sir, the sun will be up any minute. As soon as I can see the runway, we are off. Please, can you man the three machine guns in the fishbowls?" Jason said.

"Fishbowls?" Pete asked.

"You know, the—"

"The Plexiglas domes?" Wilson asked wryly.

"Thank you," Jason mumbled. "Just please sit in there and use

176

the guns if we get shot at. Once I turn this thing on, it will wake up the entire island." He limped toward the cockpit.

"Jason, have you tested the engines? Will it start?" Wilson asked.

Jason shrugged. "Let's hope so. The battery indicator is at 75 percent. It's full of fuel. I hope it starts. I have already removed the wheel chucks."

"Have you flown a plane…before?" Wilson asked. He stumbled over the words, betraying his nervousness.

"Not exactly, sir."

"Not exactly?" Pete asked.

"I've flown in a simulator," Jason admitted.

"That's all?" John gasped.

"Can any of you fly?" Jason snapped back.

Nobody said a word. Finally, Wilson cleared his throat. "That's good enough for me. Move!"

Jason made his way to the cockpit. Major Wilson climbed into the Plexiglas dome on the plane's rear. Pete climbed a small steel ladder up into the revolving dome on the top of the plane. Ryan climbed into the dome below that hung down from the plane's belly. John joined him to help him reload.

After he painfully eased himself down into the pilot's seat, Jason strapped on the headphones and turned on the power.

A thin line of orange on the eastern horizon told him that daybreak was near. He could barely make out the runway in the darkness. He pulled the four engine throttles back slightly and fired engines one and two. To his relief, they both started and kicked into action. He repeated the process with three and four. With all four engines running, he pulled back on the throttle. The huge sleeping giant roared. The sound carried with the wind for miles across the flat landscape. Inside the plane, the racket was deafening. Jason released the brakes. Nothing happened.

"Come on. Go," he hissed.

Still nothing. He increased the revs and slowly the plane lurched forward. As he used the rudders and tiller, he turned to face the runway. After he took a deep breath, he placed the brake back on and opened the throttles on all four engines.

The truck-sized Boeing engines roared. The B-24 rattled and shook. Jason knew he had to get the engines running at a high speed before he released the brakes again. He had only ever flown a small propeller plane in a simulator. He had normally just used the jets to practice on.

"Good luck, Steed!" Wilson shouted. "God speed!"

Jason released the brake. The plane lurched forward and started to gather speed. He increased the throttle and increased the speed. Lights from a vehicle came on ahead. The sirens had gone off, and the guards poured out of the barracks. Jason slowly pulled back on the tiller. Nothing happened; the plane just continued down the runway.

It bounced and rattled its way toward the buildings. He gave it more power. Still nothing happened when he tried to lift the wheels off the ground for takeoff. The buildings were now getting close. The plane felt lighter to control but would not clear the buildings. He cut power and applied the brakes.

The plane slowed and bounced to a stop. They were now desperately close to the barracks and Weing's armed guards. Again, he opened the throttles and slowly turned around. He applied the brakes and opened the throttles again. The back of the plane started taking shots from behind.

"Jason! *Go! Go!*" Wilson shouted as he turned the rear machine guns on the oncoming guards. Both Ryan and Peter in their Plexiglas domes turned to the rear and also began shooting.

The tail began receiving heavy fire. The armored jeeps were getting closer and closer. The second jeep had a mounted machine gun and started firing at the plane. Wilson targeted this vehicle and unloaded his rounds. The driver and gunman were killed instantly, and the jeep veered off to the left and turned over, bursting into flames.

Wilson was screaming at the top of his voice for Jason to move, but the noise of the engines drowned any sound he made. Jason pulled the throttles farther back. The plane's old body shook violently.

"This baby is going to need everything to get it off the ground," he said to himself.

He applied more throttle and still held it. Eventually, he released the brakes.

The plane launched forward. He pulled the throttle back farther and farther. With its 110-foot wingspan bouncing, the B-24 stormed down the runway. Now that it was going faster than it was before, it felt even lighter to control. Jason opened the throttles all the way. He wanted to get as much speed as possible. He pulled back the tiller. The end of the runway and the wire fence rushed toward him. He had to go now. He was going too fast to stop.

The thirty-three ton plane slowly lifted off the ground and roared into the cloudless dawn sky. Wilson, John, Ryan, and Pete started cheering as they left the complex behind.

Jason turned on the radio to call for help.

"This is Jason Steed of the 22nd Platoon Sea Cadets, requesting flight information—over."

The signal was picked up by the HMS *Ark Royal*, the HMS *Stoke*, Scott Turner, the admiralty, and, unfortunately, the Chinese.

═

Back in London, Scott screamed to his mother to come and listen. When she came running into his room, the message was repeated. Scott hugged her and jumped up and down, punching the air.

═

Ray was on the bridge, and he could not believe his ears. The sweet unbroken voice of his son came loud and clear over the airways. The bridge crew members cheered and gave Ray a pat on the back. Ray had to fight back his emotions.

"This is Jason Steed of the 22nd Platoon Sea Cadets, requesting flight information—over," Jason repeated over the radio.

"G'day. Jason Steed, this is Broom Air Force Base Northwestern Australia. Roger Bankman speaking. Please give your position—over."

"I have no idea, sir. Somewhere over Jakarta, flying SW, 22 degrees—over."

"We have you on radar. What are you flying, Jason?" Roger replied.

"I don't know, sir. A big American World War II bomber. It has four engines, three domes. It's green, noisy, and bloody huge, sir."

The officers on the bridge of the *Ark Royal*, including Ray, fell about, laughing. Then, a new voice came over the airways.

"This is Commander Elliot from special forces. Jason Steed, we got your message."

"What message, sir?"

"Are you still in a position to trade for some carrot cake?"

"Wow! You got that. Yes, sir, I want to trade."

"Then, Jason, keep heading toward Broom Airfield. Someone will meet you there."

═══

Wilson made his way to the cockpit and sat next to Jason in the navigator's seat. He put on a pair of headphones to hear what Jason could hear. A tired grin crossed his face.

"Jason, head two degrees south," Commander Elliot instructed. "You are approximately forty-five minutes from us. How is your fuel?"

"It's just below 60 percent, sir," Jason replied. "We are leaving Jakarta. I can see the coastline below us."

"You have enough. Just keep it steady."

"Aye, aye, sir."

Easier said than done, Jason thought. It took every ounce of strength he had to fight the controls, although he didn't want to show Wilson how much he was struggling. He eased the plane toward the Australian coast. The sun shone directly into the cockpit, blinding Jason's vision to his right. Below, the sun sparkled off the Indian Ocean.

"I can see the *Ark Royal* on the horizon on our right," Wilson announced, squinting.

"Jason, this is Commander Elliot again. Are you speaking to Major Wilson?"

"He certainly was. Hello, commander," Wilson said.

"It's great to hear your voice again, Wilson. How did you get out? What about the others?"

"Jason got us out. Pete, Ryan, and young John Leigh. This was after he achieved the mission's objective."

Nobody said a word.

"Well done, Sea Cadet Steed," Commander Elliot finally commented.

Wilson switched off the headphones and looked at Jason.

"What?" Jason asked.

"Listen…I know you feel bad about the guards you killed, but let me tell you something, Jason. You did a good job—no, a bloody good job. I take it as a sea cadet that you will one day want to join the marines or join the navy. You already have what it takes to join special ops. You will be SAS material, but I know what killing can do to a man. What I mean to say is…you have friends in the service now—"

A raspy Cantonese voice cut off Wilson in mid-sentence.

"This is the People's Republic of China. You are in our airspace. You must return immediately or you will be shot down."

"Broom Airfield, did you hear that?" Jason asked.

"We got it and are going to get it translated—"

"I understood it. It said we are in Chinese airspace, and we are to return or get shot down," Jason said.

Wilson gestured out the window. Jason could see two Chinese helicopters in the distance.

"Broom Airfield, Commander Elliot please, what do I do?" Jason asked, concerned.

"Keep going, Jason. We have dispatched an escort. The ETA is seven minutes," Elliot replied.

"This is Broom Airfield. Be advised that the Chinese are just one minute away," Bankman instructed.

Jason pulled back on the throttle to increase the speed. Major Wilson ran to the back of the plane and climbed into the rear Plexiglas dome to man the machine guns.

"People's Republic of China, this is the pilot," Jason announced in Cantonese. "Please be advised we are an American plane and in Australian airspace. Stand down."

There was no response. The first helicopter fired a few warning shots. The huge bomber had not been built for speed or maneuverability. It had been built for dropping bombs.

"We need some help now!" Jason shouted.

A second wave of shots came at the plane, and Wilson opened fire with his machine guns. The helicopter withdrew but retaliated by firing its air-to-air missile. It missed but exploded near the bottom of the plane. The whole plane shook violently. The left inside engine caught fire.

"We have taken a direct hit. One of the engines is on fire. We need some help—now," Jason begged.

"Steed, turn off that engine," Commander Elliot barked. "That will cut the fuel, and the fire should go out. You can fly on three engines without a payload."

Jason's eyes darted across the control panel. He flicked the switch to the fuel on engine three. A shaky sigh of relief escaped his lips as the flames flickered and vanished.

"The fire is out, but it's hard to keep level now."

"Jason, stay calm—"

A wave of gunfire tore into the cockpit, shattering the glass to his right. Jason cried out in pain as something searing hot tore into his stomach. Wind screamed in his ear. The plane tilted to the left and started to descend.

"Jason Steed, this is Broom Airfield. You are losing altitude. Please maintain 1,000 meters. Pull up. Pull up."

Jason stared down in horror at his belly. "I have been shot. I… Blood is everywhere," he croaked. Even through his panic, however, he could see that he'd just been strafed. The bullet had grazed him, not entered his body.

"Pull back on the tiller," the voice from Broom Airfield shouted. "You are going to fall into a dive. You must pull up."

Out of the corner of his dimming eyes, Jason spotted two Royal Navy helicopters. Before he knew what was happening, both Chinese helicopters exploded in fireballs off to his right. He was too light-headed to focus. He tried to reach out to grasp the tiller, but he stopped short as his stomach clenched in agony.

"Jason, you need to pull up; come on, son, pull her up," Roger repeated. Jason's microphone came back on. His voice was breaking; he paused and struggled between words.

"I tried. I can't do anymore…I can't do it…I tried." Jason coughed.

Scott's tears of joy turned to tears of pain, as he heard his friend crying in pain. Roger said no more; he knew he could not push the kid any further. The plane continued to fall.

Lieutenant Commander Raymond Steed took a deep breath.

His captain and colleagues watched him as the teary-eyed lieutenant picked up the radio microphone on the *Ark Royal's* bridge. He knew he had to try something to get his son to respond, no matter how hard it was.

"Jason, this is Lieutenant Commander Steed. Can you hear me, son?" After a small pause, Jason replied, "Dad…I…I tried. I can't do it anymore. I did. I did try."

"Jason, was it your idea to fly the plane back?"

"Yes," he choked out.

"You have put four men on that plane at risk. You also have something that we need. Don't you dare let us down now. Wake up and pull yourself together. Listen to control and pull the plane back up. Do you hear me?"

Captain Stephens was shocked at Ray's harsh words to his son. Scott was still in his bedroom, listening with his mother. His mouth dropped in disbelief. Some of the crew in the bridge had tears in their eyes as they watched Ray struggle with his emotions. Ray took a breath and squeezed the microphone hard; his knuckles turned white as he forced himself to push his son. No reply came from Jason. The plane continued to fall.

"Jason, did you hear what I said? Pull yourself together and get a bloody grip!" Steed said, not knowing if this was the last time he would speak to his son.

Jason closed his eyes, took a deep breath, gritted his teeth, and dug deeper than he ever had before. His father was right. Lives were at stake—lives that weren't his to bargain with. He blinked rapidly. The massive old bomber was now probably less than 200 meters above ground. Again, he tried once more to reach the tiller;

he ignored the incredible pain as his injured stomach muscles contracted and pulled it back. "I am going to turn engine three on again. I need the power to pull out of the dive," Jason said.

The two-ton, turbocharged engine roared back to life. The plane shook and bounced violently as Jason fought with the controls.

"The engine's on fire again. I'll turn it off," he reported. His breathing changed to panting. His body was cold and losing blood rapidly. He could see the airfield ahead of him, near the coastline. It swam dizzily before his bleary eyes.

"What fuel do you have left, son?" Roger asked.

"Ten percent, sir."

Wilson joined Jason back in the cockpit. He winced when he saw Jason covered in blood and glass. "Okay, Jason, I don't think you have enough for two attempts. We have to get it right the first time. Lower your landing gear."

Jason painfully lifted himself forward and released the crank. There was a terrible rending noise, and black sludge squirted from an area on the floor. The suffocating odor of gasoline filled the cockpit.

"It's not working. Oil is shooting up from the floor," Wilson cried, panic creeping into his voice. "The missile must have damaged the landing gear."

There was a pause from the control tower.

"Wong Tong says always look further than what you can see," Jason quoted, feeling suddenly and strangely calm.

"What the bloody hell does that mean?" Wilson shrieked. "Who the hell is Wong Tong?"

Jason almost smiled. "We don't need wheels. We can make an emergency landing. I've trained on it."

Wilson gaped out the window.

"Jason, are you all right?" Roger's voice crackled through the headset. "I need to know that you're clearheaded—"

"Sorry, sir, I have to turn off the radio. I need to concentrate. The mission objective is stuffed down my underwear. Pete, Ryan, John, get to the cockpit and strap yourselves in!"

Jason clicked off the radio. He heard frightened muttering behind him as the three others buckled themselves into the emergency jump seats. As he summoned every last ounce of strength he had, Jason willed himself awake, alert, and focused. The runway leveled off in front of him, just as it had countless times on the simulator, but landing without gear meant that he had to keep the plane as level as possible with the runway. Seconds slowed to an agonizing crawl as the plane descended and descended, and at the last possible moment, he nudged the nose forward.

"Jason, no!" Wilson cried.

The bottom Plexiglas dome was the first thing to hit the ground, crushed instantly like a wet paper cup. A propeller hit the ground, smashing it to pieces and causing the plane to veer off the runway at terrific speed. Another prop hit the ground, sending shards of metal as high as fifty feet in the air. Sparks, dust, and flames followed the plane. Jason squeezed his eyes shut and gripped the tiller as tightly as he could. A wing tore off, sending the remaining plane into a spin, tearing up the runway and grass. Sparks and debris flew in all directions from the plane's twisted and ruptured body as it rumbled to a halt.

Jason blinked. He was alive.

"You did it!" Wilson shouted. "You bloody did it!"

Too stunned to move, Jason simply stared out the window.

Sirens sounded as emergency crews sped to the scene.

"The plane is on fire. Get them out!" a voice shouted over the radio. "Get them out—"

The last thing Jason remembered clearly was the smell of smoke. Disjointed images floated through his mind: a masked paramedic hauling him onto a stretcher, the bright blue sky above him, and Wilson's voice shouting, "That's no little kid. That's Jason Steed, the biggest damn hero you will ever see!"

Chapter Sixteen

BACK IN LONDON, THE queen received a phone call from Prime Minister Harold Wilson.

"Ma'am, we have some good news. In fact, good news all around. We have recovered what was stolen in Australia. While we speak, they are disarming the missile," he explained.

"Does one have any news on the prisoners?" she asked.

"Yes, ma'am, they have been rescued and are all alive."

"How delightful. Well done, Prime Minister. I have to ask, as he is a friend of my daughter's. Has the missing Sea Cadet Jason Steed's body been recovered yet?"

"Jason Steed was responsible for the recovery of the cassette and hatched the escape plan for our prisoners. He also flew the prisoners back."

"I don't think we are talking about the same person, Prime Minister. Jason Steed is just a small boy."

"No, ma'am, it is the same person. He is a young sea cadet that got caught up in the mission after the attack. However, he is in critical condition. I will have my staff keep you posted on his condition, but...it does not look hopeful."

"Thank you, Mr. Wilson." The queen hung up and debated how to break the news to her daughter.

＝

Jason's torn and tattered body arrived at the hospital and was rushed to the trauma ward. He was given over five pints of blood. A team of doctors sewed up his stomach. During surgery, he suffered heart failure because of blood loss, and he fell into a coma. They worked on him for four hours as his father waited.

Ray hated hospitals. They brought back memories of when Karen had died. And now to think he might lose his son—

Finally, a doctor emerged from the ER. He was an Indian man in his fifties wearing thick black-rimmed glasses. "I am Dr. Gupta, Mr. Steed. Your son has suffered. His tiny body has been through a meat grinder. I don't really know where to start, so let me start from the bottom up."

Ray nodded. "If he's alive, that's all that matters."

"Okay then. His feet are covered in blisters and sores, and some are infected. He treated a bullet wound to his leg himself. It will heal, but the muscle is damaged. As far as the stomach wound goes…well, he has very dense stomach muscles. This probably saved his life. He must be very active in sports to be built like this at such a young age. He could make a recovery from this. His upper body is covered in mosquito bites, cuts, and bruises. He has two broken fingers. His small finger is broken in three places. I don't think his heart is damaged. His face has cuts on his cheek, forehead, nose, bottom lip, and chin. He has a black eye, and his right ear was cut badly. We removed glass from it."

"But…he's alive," Ray said, trying to process it all.

"He is alive but in a coma. His body has gone through hell. On top of that, he is very malnourished. This is just the physical damage. He stopped breathing for a short period. We are hoping he does not have brain damage. We have him on a drip, a monitor, and we are trying to do everything we can to keep him alive. It's up to him now, but I don't think he has anymore to give." He opened his mouth, as if he was going to add something, but then shut it.

"What is it?" Ray asked.

Dr. Gupta peered at him over the rims of his glasses. "If he does survive, the emotional scars he'll bear will take a lifetime to heal. What the hell were you doing using a kid on a mission in a war zone?"

"I—" Ray could not answer. His eyes filled with tears.

"I understand. It wasn't your decision. You may see your son now."

Dr. Gupta led him into the ER. Ray could hardly breathe. Jason looked so tiny, surrounded by monitors, tubes, and machines. His skin was pale, and he'd lost so much weight. Most of his body was covered in dressings and splints. Ray knelt down heavily on the floor next to Jason's bed and wept. He gently held Jason's right hand and prayed for God's help.

===

Crash. Bang.

What was that?

Jason licked his dry lips. Voices? Yes. In English—but with an accent. Was it American? No, it was Australian.

Jason lay for a long while with his eyes closed, listening to the sounds of footsteps and doors opening and closing. He slowly opened his eyes; however, the brightness of the sun made him squint. The ceiling was white. He slowly tried to raise himself on one elbow, but he was immediately hit by a bolt of pain in his stomach. His throat was dry, and his lungs burned. He lay back down. He then became aware of someone breathing to his right. He turned his head and could make out the shape of his father asleep in the chair next to him. He was unshaved, and he looked pale.

After he mustered the biggest breath he could, Jason croaked, "Where's my carrot cake?"

A smile of disbelief crossed Ray's face, and his eyes bulged. He jumped up and shouted for the doctors. Dr. Gupta rushed in and spent the next hour examining him.

"The boy is like a young eagle—a fledgling with the heart of a lion," he pronounced.

$$=$$

Three days later, Jason was back home in London. He was confined to bed, of course, but after he was home just an hour, Jason requested that his father phone Scott's parents to ask if Scott could come and see him. Within five minutes, the entire Turner family was at the Steeds' door. Scott didn't bother to knock first. He simply dashed in, bolted up the stairs, and burst into Jason's room.

"Hey, Scott," Jason said, smiling. He propped himself up on some pillows. His father leaned over to help.

Scott took one look at him and said, "You look like a dehydrated zombie. I knew you were superman and you would survive, but Jesus, you look terrible."

"Ha! Thanks for being honest."

Scott insisted on seeing Jason's bullet wounds.

"I am hoping they won't scar too much," Ray said, peeling back Jason's pajama jacket.

"I can help," said Dr. Turner from the doorway. "I'm a plastic surgeon. Once they heal, I'm sure I can do something with that and the scars on his leg. We have new procedures now, and we can use skin grafts. Once he matures, he will even grow hairs just like the rest of his legs."

"I would want that. I don't care what it costs," Ray said.

"Don't I get a say in this?" Jason asked with a smirk.

"Jason is part of our family. It will be an honor and won't cost you a penny," said the doctor, now looking at Jason's leg.

Mrs. Betton brought up a pot of tea and some carrot cake for the visitors.

"While you're at it, can you do anything to make Jase less ugly, Dad?" Scott joked in a deadpan voice.

Jason rolled his eyes. "You're lucky I'm bedridden. Wait until I get better. You are in for it."

Chapter Seventeen

THE FOLLOWING MORNING, RAY received an unannounced visit from Ministry of Defense Commissioner Brian Hurrel. Alone with Ray in his study, Hurrel explained that they had recommended that Jason receive the Queen's Award for Bravery. It was the same award Ray himself was awarded years earlier. However, Jason was also nominated for a Victoria Cross for outstanding bravery in the rescue of Major Wilson, John Leigh, Peter Tucker, and Ryan Lentz. He went on to say that the following Tuesday, the queen was formally handing out honors. The press would be there, and if Jason was well enough, she would like him to attend.

"In a situation like this, we should ask him," Ray said.

"Well, he's not going to say no. Can we just say you will be there?" Hurrel said with a smile.

"No, we need to ask him. Follow me," Ray said.

They walked up the large wooden staircase to Jason's room. Ray knocked on the door, waited a few seconds, and went in. Jason was sitting up in bed, and Scott was sitting next to him. The two boys were playing chess.

"Jase, this is Brian Hurrel from the MOD. You are going to be honored with a VC and Queen's Award for Bravery. It's next Tuesday. I can get you a new uniform. Do you want to go?"

Jason exchanged an excited glance with Scott. He shook Hurrel's hand. "Will there be TV cameras and newspaper people?"

Hurrel chuckled. "Sure. You will be on TV. The youngest person ever to get a VC and to get the Queen's Award."

"Then, I don't want to go. Tell them thanks, but I did not do it for a medal."

Scott nearly fell off his chair. He put his hand to Jason's forehead. "Are you feeling all right, mate? The girls are gonna love this—I mean, not that you should do it for that, but—"

Jason shook his head and sighed. "I don't want to be on TV. I just want to be normal. If I do this, when we go back to school, everyone will stare. I don't want that. No, I would rather not—thanks."

Hurrel's smile became strained. "But this is a great honor. You can't turn it down."

"It was nice to get asked…but no," Jason replied.

Ray said nothing. He had decided to let Jason make up his own mind.

"Okay, Jason," Hurrel said. "What if we arrange a private ceremony? Just you and two family members? We can do it after the press has gone. We'll say it's for an unnamed military person. We do this on rare occasions for the SAS." The sound of being treated just like the SAS made Jason's eyes light up.

"Five family members, and I will do it," Jason said.

"Good heavens, you want it all, don't you?" Hurrel replied.

"Is it a deal?" Jason said, holding out his hand.

"For anyone else, no, but for you, yes," he said and shook Jason's hand. "I will make the arrangements, and I will show myself out—thank you."

"Five family members? We don't have five, do we?" Ray asked, looking at Jason with his eyebrows raised.

"Uncle Stewart, Nana and Grandpa Macintosh, you, and Scott. Imagine how excited they will be when we call them and tell them. Grandpa does not stop talking about the last time he met the queen at Balmoral. He will love it."

———

That night, Jason had his first nightmare.

He dreamed he and Todd were on the beach. Again, the two shots hit Todd, pulling him away from Jason's grip. He tried to hang on but could not. He woke himself up after he shouted Todd's name, sweating and panting.

Ray ran into Jason's room and turned on the light. "What is it, son?"

"It's nothing. I was having a bad dream. I keep seeing Todd's face and his eyes looking at me."

Ray sat down and hugged him.

"Am I going to get these dreams a lot?" Jason asked.

"I hope not, son. Do you ever think of the people you killed? Or the others in your team who died?"

"No, the ones I killed, I just did what I had to do. I remember seeing Jim dead, but Todd was looking right at me when his eyes just went lifeless."

"I can get you some help if you need it," Ray murmured.

Jason shook his head. "I can take it…I think."

"I used to see your mother's face when she was lying in the hospital. Eventually, it fades. I am sure this will get better. Once you get new memories, the old ones will fade. But if you ever need to talk to me, I am always here. There's no shame in asking for help."

=

On the day of the ceremony, Uncle Stewart swore his uniform had shrunk at the cleaners. It was too tight around his middle. Scott wore a new suit his mother had bought for the occasion. Jason's grandparents wore their Sunday's best clothes. Jason wore his Sea Cadet uniform. His left arm was still in a sling, and his hand was bandaged. He walked with a slight limp, but the doctors assured him it would go away once he started exercising again.

When he came down the stairs wearing his uniform, his father stopped and stared.

"What?" Jason asked.

"I have never seen you in uniform before. You look so grown up...and as I am in uniform, you know you should salute me," Ray teased.

Jason grinned. "That will never happen. Here, in this house, you are just Dad."

"Will you grow your hair long again at the front?" Ray asked.

"If I can get away with it. If not, it's no big deal."

The rest of the morning passed in a blur. All Jason could think about was seeing Catherine again. When they arrived at Buckingham Palace, members of the secret service ushered them into a large deserted room packed with chairs. Jason and the others sat and exchanged puzzled shrugs.

The door at the back opened, and the queen entered. With her was another man in a suit carrying a blue velvet cushion. Two others followed. She stood at the center of the stage. A footman gestured Jason to come forward. As he did, he noticed Catherine in the corner. He broke into a wide smile. Then, he bowed his head.

The queen began to speak: "Our country owes you a great debt. You have showed great bravery and courage in the rescue and support of fellow Sea Cadet Todd Johnson. I hereby award you the Queen's Award for Bravery. I would also like to award you the Victoria Cross. This is our country's highest award for bravery. You showed great courage and bravery in securing the release of four captured British subjects. Your country thanks you." She walked down the steps and pinned both the Queen's Award and the Victoria Cross on Jason's chest. She turned, walked back up the steps, then looked back at Jason and paused. "Master Steed, in this instance, I have something to add."

Jason looked up at the queen.

"I understand you have been writing to my daughter, Catherine. This has to stop."

For the briefest instant, Jason was tempted to tear the medals off his chest and hurl them into the queen's face, but then the old lady smiled.

"I don't want you to write to her anymore. I would prefer it if you started seeing each other again."

Ignoring all protocol, Jason ran over to Catherine and swept her into a hug.

====

On Thursday, Jason dressed in his Sea Cadet uniform and asked his father to drive him to Liverpool. They stopped at the address the admiralty had given him. Two boys played football in the street, and a small group of girls played hopscotch on the pavement. The houses were all the same. The only difference between them was that each of the front doors was painted different colors.

"Do you want me to come in, Jason?" Ray asked.

"No, I need to do this alone," Jason said, picking up a blue velvet box. "But thanks, Dad."

"I'll be waiting here in the car then."

The children stopped playing and watched Jason walk up to the house. He knocked hard on the brass knocker. A girl, aged about fifteen, opened the door and looked at Jason.

"Oh, my god, I thought you were someone else. Can I help you?"

"Is your mum home? I am a friend of Todd's."

The girl nodded mutely, and Jason followed her down the thin hallway. Todd's mother sat in the corner on a couch watching the TV. She was a plump lady with a round, reddish face. She had dark brown hair that was gray at the roots.

In the center of the room against one wall was a small gas fire on a brown-tiled fireplace. The mantelpiece was full of sympathy cards. In the center of the chimney hung a large picture of Todd, probably his last school photo.

"Mum, it's a friend of Todd's," the girl murmured. "He wants to see you."

Without looking up, she replied, "I can't deal with him. Ask him to come back."

The room went silent. She then slowly looked up and saw Jason standing at the doorway to her living room and said, "Oh, I am so sorry." She swallowed and pushed herself to stand up, but Jason shook his head and waved her back down. "You must be Jason?" she continued. "The last letter I got from Todd...he wrote that you were friends. The admiralty told me his friend helped him to shore and up the beach—was that you?"

Jason opened his mouth, but the words died in his throat. Seeing the tiny home, seeing how much Todd's mother and sister resembled his friend—he couldn't take it. His eyes welled up, and tears ran down his cheeks. His bottom lip quivered.

Todd's mother held out her welcoming arms. He ran to her and hugged her. For the first time since Todd had died, Jason cried uncontrollably. She kissed his head.

"I'm sorry. I didn't want to get like this," Jason said, weeping.

She wiped his tears with her fingers. "Thank you for trying to save him. He liked you. He wrote and told me how you helped him get over his homesickness."

"I want you to have this." Jason sniffed, passing her the Queen's Award for Bravery.

She blinked at it, her eyes moistening. "I can't take this. It's yours. You deserve it."

"I can't get him out of my head. I can still see him looking at me when he—" Jason paused. "You know—Please keep it. Todd was a hero and a good friend of mine. He loved all his family. I knew I would be welcomed by you."

Todd's mother squeezed his hand. "You are welcome here any time, Jason. I hope you can get over the trauma."

Jason nodded in thanks, hugged her again, and quickly hurried toward the door.

"Wait!" his sister called. She bolted up the stairs and came back down with a handful of martial arts magazines. "Take these please. I know Todd would have wanted you to have them. They'll just go to waste here."

Jason swallowed and took them. "Thanks," he croaked.

His father kept quiet as Jason settled into the front seat and sniffled.

"I'm proud of you, son," Ray said gently, passing him a tissue. "That's not an easy thing you just did."

Jason nodded. "I feel better now. I will write to them. They are nice people. Look, they gave me a couple of karate magazines. Todd never got to read these."

"You'll keep his memory alive," his father said as they drove down the street.

Jason flicked through the glossy pages. "Wow, Jet Chan has become the Under-Eighteen World Karate Champion," he read out loud.

"This Jet Chan—do you know him?"

"Yes, I fought him in a competition in Hong Kong. He does jujitsu."

"How did you do when you fought him?"

Jason grinned, and for the first time since he'd been home, he felt almost normal. "What do you think that big trophy was for?"

Chapter Eighteen

THE DAY BEFORE RAY was to return to the HMS *Ark Royal* for another long tour, he told Jason he was taking him out for a meal—just the two of them. Jason got dressed up in shirt and tie and waited for his father to return from his trip into the city. When he saw his father's car pulling into the driveway, he shouted bye to Mrs. Betton and slammed the door behind him. Then, he stopped short. His father wasn't alone. Two other people were in the car. Scott was in the front seat, and Catherine was sitting in the back.

"Surprise!" his dad, Scott, and Catherine shouted at once.

"How did you get Catherine away without the secret service?" Jason gasped.

"It wasn't easy, but as long as we stay together, we are fine," Ray explained.

Jason jumped in the back with Catherine. He leaned forward and squeezed his dad's shoulder. "Thanks, Dad. Where are we going?"

"There's a pub I know not far from here. It serves great food, and hopefully, it'll be dark enough so that nobody will recognize our special guest." He smiled at Catherine in the rearview mirror.

Within minutes, they were snaking their way through a series of winding country lanes. Rain began to patter on the roof as darkness fell. Every so often, Catherine leaned over to tickle Jason. He couldn't stop giggling.

"Ouch. That's my wound. Stop it!"

Suddenly, Ray slowed.

A car was idling in the middle of the road ahead, blocking their direction. As they drew closer, Jason noticed two men in dark rain-coats standing on either side of the vehicle.

Ray stopped about twenty feet away from the car and the two strange men. The windshield wipers thumped in the silence.

"I'll go and see what's up."

Ray opened his door to get out, and Scott grabbed his arm. "I don't think you should get out. They may be after someone," Scott whispered.

"Not us. We have not done anything wrong," Ray said, trying to reassure Scott.

"I know, but we have Catherine in the back," Scott said. Jason exchanged a quick glance with Catherine. "Dad, turn the car around. Let's go another way just in case."

Ray nodded, closed his door, and reversed the car back. Jason looked behind. Another car had appeared out of nowhere and screeched to a stop behind them.

We're trapped, Jason thought.

Three men got out. One was heavyset and dressed in a light-colored trench coat. He sat on the front hood of the car and lit a cigarette, shielding the lighter to protect it from the rain. One of his companions opened an umbrella over his head. Ray glanced back at Jason.

Jason flung his door open. "Dad, just promise me you will stay in the car with Catherine and Scott. If you get a chance, just go."

"Jason, get back in now!" Ray shouted.

After he slammed the door behind him, Jason strode forward toward the three men. He removed his left arm from the sling and dropped the sling to the ground. He slowly clenched his right fist.

After a few seconds of silence, the man with the cigarette stubbed it out and slowly clapped his hands in applause.

"You got guts, Steed. I read your profile. Bloody impressive. Queen's Award for Bravery, Victoria Cross, and now you get out of a car with a hand in a cast, and you are prepared to fight us. I knew you were right for the job. Let me introduce myself. I'm George Young. I am a commander for the undercover intelligence unit for SYUI."

"SYUI? What's that?"

"Scotland Yard Undercover Intel."

"What do you want with us?"

"It's you I want. I need your help with a job."

"Hang on a second. All this—men in dark suits on a country lane—just to ask me something? You scared the life out of us."

"Sorry if I upset your family. I just wanted to see your reaction. You did all right, son."

"If you know so much about me, you know where I live. If you want to ask me something, come to my house in an hour. Let me take my friends home first."

Jason turned and started to walk toward his father's car.

"Steed, it's me that calls the shots here, not you," the man called after him.

As he bent down to pick up his sling, Jason replied, "One hour. Take it or leave it. I'm taking my friends home first." He climbed in the back, his heartbeat slowing down. He realized all at once that he was dripping wet. The others all stared at him.

"His name is George Young, and he says he is from SYUI," Jason said, slipping his arm back into its sling. "Have you heard of that?"

His father nodded and eyed the cars suspiciously as they disappeared into the night, leaving them alone once again on the country road.

"He knows my name and wants me to do a job for him."

"What job?" Scott asked.

"I didn't ask. I told him to come to our house in an hour. He can ask you, Dad. I have no idea what sort of job." Jason took a deep breath. "I'm sorry. I guess this ruins our dinner plans. We could order in though."

"What is SYUI?" Scott asked.

"Scotland Yard Undercover Intelligence Department," Catherine said.

Jason and the others all raised their eyebrows.

She laughed. "Well, I do have a policeman with me most of the time, and I have ears. Don't look so surprised. What do they want you for? You're shaking. Are you all right?" she asked, taking his hand.

"I am now—thanks," Jason replied.

Ray looked at Catherine. "I'm sorry, Princess Catherine, but I believe it's best if I take you home now."

"Of course," she said.

Nobody said a word after that. Jason kept a tight hold of Catherine's hand the entire ride back into London. Ray dropped Catherine off with a guard at the entrance to Buckingham Palace and then dropped Scott off at his house. When they finally pulled into the driveway of their home nearly an hour later, Ray let out a deep sigh. "SYUI will be here any second."

Jason nodded. "I'll go ask Mrs. Betton to put some tea on—"

"Wait." Ray bit his lip. "You and Catherine seem…tight."

"Tight?" Jason asked, puzzled.

"Yes, tight, you know…close."

"I suppose we are."

Ray nodded. "Just…be careful, son. You're very young, and she's royalty."

"I don't care. She makes me laugh. That's what matters."

His father laughed softly. "I know exactly what you mean. I felt the exact same way about your mother."

A pair of headlights pulled up behind them, ending the conversation. Ray sighed again and hurried to open the door for George Young. Jason climbed out of the car, relieved that Mr. Young had come alone this time. He closed the door behind the three of them, and they stood dripping in the hallway.

"Here we go. Here's my card," George Young said in a thick cockney accent. He passed it to Ray, who snatched it and folded his arms across his chest.

"What the hell is your problem?" Ray snapped. "I had another two his age and size in the car with me tonight when you thought you would play gangsters. What sort of idiot are you? You scared them and me and spoiled our evening."

The pudgy man chuckled, stinking of cigarette smoke. "I suppose I deserved that."

"What is it you want?" Ray demanded.

George Young smiled. "Mind if I smoke?"

"Yes, I do. Tell us what you want," Ray snapped.

"Right then. I like the direct type." He turned to Jason and continued, "We got this Triad gang in North London, see. They are like the mafia, but these geezers are Asian. They sell drugs, cigarettes, booze—anything they can nick. They use a small army. Well, I call 'em teenage Bruce Lees. They wear black clothing, masks, and break in and steal everything that ain't bleeding tied down."

Ray cleared his throat. "What does that have to do with my son?"

George Young kept his eyes on Jason. "These teenagers are deadly, and they're expecting a shipment of drugs. It will be cheap and have half the bloody city addicted. We need a guy right on the inside. This geezer, Andrew Cho, is fifteen. He's currently in juvie and has four months on his sentence to go. He is the son of Lin Cho, the Triad leader. We need Jason to befriend Cho in juvie and find out about the shipment… oh, and one more thing. We know Andrew Cho could be a target himself by a rival group."

Ray gaped at him. Finally, he started to laugh.

"This is funny to you?" George Young asked.

"It is, in fact. You want me to send Jason to a youth detention center. You want him to befriend a fifteen-year-old drug lord's son and find out about a drug shipment, not forgetting someone may try and bump this kid off?"

Young shrugged. "You got it in one. I can arrange for him to share a cell with Andrew Cho."

"No. No way will I allow that. He's eleven. He's still not fully recovered, and he has done his bit for his country. He goes to one of the best schools in London. It's out of the question to send him to jail."

Jason opened his mouth to say something but then thought better of it.

"Look, Steed, we're on the same side 'ere, but we need someone who can use martial arts. If he becomes friends with Cho, when they are released, Cho will want Jason with his skills on his side. Well, they don't come any better than him, do they? We need someone young who won't be suspected. We need someone who wants to work undercover for the SAS one day and someone who can think on his feet. Well, he's proved that, right?" He looked over at Jason and winked.

"The answer is still no. Forget it," Ray said firmly.

"Suit yourself. You have my card if you change your mind. I'll show myself out."

With that, the pudgy man waddled over to the door and slammed it shut behind him.

For a several moments, Jason and his father stood silently in the hall, staring at each other.

"Life will never be the same for you, son," his father muttered at long last.

"I know," Jason said. "Dad?"

"Yes?"

"Do you think George Young will be back if we don't get in touch with him first?"

Ray laughed and put his arm around Jason's shoulder, steering him toward the kitchen. "Oh, I'm certain of it, but we'll worry about that later. Let's finally get that dinner, shall we?"

The adventure continues in

Fledgling

Revenge of Boudicca

Coming soon...

Chapter One

THE YAMAHA RD 250 motorcycle circled the end of Tower Hill Terrace. For the would-be thief, it would be a case of being in the wrong place at the wrong time that Saturday morning. It was the rider's bad luck that one of the people in line was eleven-year-old Jason Steed.

Princess Catherine stood in line with Jason. She wore a knitted red hat and glasses so the hundreds of tourists that surrounded them at the Tower of London would not recognize her.

Slowly the long line moved forward. Some of the excited tourists took photographs of the historic buildings. A Yeoman Warder, dressed in a smart purple and red uniform and carrying a large spear-shaped mace with a polished solid silver point, walked passed. Commonly known as beefeaters and traditionally responsible for guarding the crown jewels as well as prisoners, the Yeoman Warders were now little more than tourist guides. Many in the line quickly took a picture of him. The Yeoman smiled and rolled on his heels to his toes as he posed for photographs.

"This line is hardly moving," Catherine complained, leaning heavily on Jason. "It will take at least another twenty minutes to get in at this rate."

"Well this is what *normal* people do," Jason replied. "Now, if you want to take off your glasses and hat and let everyone see who you are and walk to the front, go ahead." He grinned.

She narrowed her eyes and shook her head at him trying to give him a dirty look behind a smile.

The motorcyclist slowly made his way up Tower Hill Terrace. In a low gear with high revs, he removed his left hand from the handlebars, pulled close to the long line of waiting tourists, and grabbed purses off of two different women in line. He opened the throttle and pulled the motorcycle's front wheel momentarily left the ground as he accelerated. Screams and shouts caught the attention of others as he roared up the narrow street, almost knocking into some of the tourists. The line jumped quickly out of his way.

Jason had seen it and was already moving in the direction of the Yeoman Warder, who was backing away to allow a gap for the speeding motorcycle. In a single move, Jason grabbed the mace with one hand, pushed the Yeoman out of the way with the other, and jumped into the path of the motorcycle. The rider never slowed or tried to alter course; he was sure this foolish boy would move out his way. At the last second, Jason jumped clear. The onlookers never really saw what happened—it was just a blur. One second, Jason was jumping clear, and the next, a loud crack sounded as the silver tip of the mace connected between the front wheel spokes and the front forks.

The front wheel instantly locked up, and the motorcycle catapulted the rider over the handlebars and sent him sprawling across the cobblestone street. The dazed rider got to his feet and started to run. Jason took off after him and tackled him, bringing him down on the ground a second time.

The rider hit out at Jason and caught the side of his face. He kicked Jason and managed to get to his feet again.

Jason paused. The punch on the side of his face hurt, and he could feel his temper rising, but he told himself to calm down. The rider shouted obscenities and spat at Jason. That was enough to tip Jason over the edge. He leapt onto one leg and threw a mae geri kick. The kick ripped off the rider's helmet, causing the chinstrap to cut deep into his neck before the buckle broke. Jason followed with a roundhouse kick directly to the man's face.

The injured rider collapsed on the cobblestones, oozing blood from his nose and neck wound. Two policemen on nearby traffic duty ran over. The rider swore at Jason as he was escorted away in handcuffs.

Jason picked up the ladies' purses and returned them, turning red as the crowd applauded him. The Yeoman took Jason and Catherine to the front of the line and allowed them into the tower without having to pay.

"Wow, Jase, that was amazing," Catherine remarked as she proudly held his hand. "You moved so fast."

"I did it to stop you complaining. See, we don't have to wait in line now."

Catherine loved going out alone with Jason. She could forget about being a princess and the pressure associated with it. Today she was just a young, pretty girl out with her boyfriend on a visit to the Tower of London.

They later settled down on a bench and shared a bag of chips, looking out over the river Thames. Any onlooker watching the little blond-haired boy sitting and laughing with a young girl would never have guessed that in a few weeks, he would be the most wanted person in Europe. But then just seeing him there, with his arm around his girlfriend, the onlookers never could have figured the kind of kid Jason Steed was, or what was about to make it all begin.

The next day, his life took a planned change. He arrived in handcuffs at a young offenders unit—this was to be Jason's home for the next four weeks. Inside housed some of London's toughest teenage thugs, among them Andrew Cho, the son of the notorious Triad leader Lin Cho. It was Lin Cho's son who Jason was to share a cell with. His cover was that he was serving four weeks for repeat shoplifting.

═

The scenery flashed past, uninteresting as scenery nearly always becomes when seen through a grimy window of a van. The police van was noisy and dirty. Jason wondered what type of criminals had previously sat in this seat on their way to prison.

Battersea Borstal for Boys, the sign read. It was a young offenders unit for boys aged eleven to sixteen. It was September 7, 1974.

The brakes squealed as the van came to a halt. A large black metal gate opened, and the van edged its way inside. The building was dark gray with hundreds of tiny windows covered with black rusted bars. Jason could see a bell tower looming up, rising crookedly over the rooftop. Pigeons perched on the edge of the building. Over time, their excrement had stained the walls. A skinny youth aged about fourteen wearing gray overalls pushed a broom along the ground trying to push the fallen autumn leaves, his efforts fruitless due to the strong wind and light rain. The driver jumped out and opened the back doors.

"Sorry, son, you have to put these on," He held out a pair of handcuffs. "I did you a favor—you should have had them on while traveling. But you being so small—well, let's face it—I didn't think you could do me any harm." He smiled and placed the handcuffs tightly on Jason's wrists. Little did the driver know who this boy was or what he was capable of.

Jason's leg painfully came back to life as he straightened it. He had been kneeling so he could see out the window. He climbed out the back of the van feeling his wrists where he would normally have worn his boys size Rolex. George Young had told him to give it to Jason's friend Scott Turner to look after as they said good-bye at SYUI headquarters. Young was a commander of Scotland Yard Undercover Intelligence Unit, or SYUI. He was leading the investigation and had put pressure on Jason to help by going undercover.

As Jason looked at his surroundings, the wind chased through his blond hair and the spray danced in his eyes. He followed the driver through a large dark door that led to a courtyard with cloisters on two sides and two bell towers rising up from the others. They went through another door. Inside it smelled of disinfectant. The driver removed Jason's handcuffs, and a tall balding prison guard gestured Jason to follow him down a corridor. Sounds of boys shouting, laughing, and cursing could be heard as they walked.

"Get undressed and take a shower and don't be all day, lad," the guard instructed. He gave Jason a plastic bag for his clothes. Jason was pleasantly surprised to find the shower water warm. The guard lit a cigarette and watched him.

"What are those marks on your stomach and leg? Have you been burnt?" he asked.

"Yes, sir, but it's nearly healed now," Jason replied quietly.

The truth was that Jason had just come out of plastic surgery, having had the two bullet wounds surgically covered. He knew he was going to be forced to tell a lot more lies before the next four weeks were over.

"Okay, that's enough. I ain't got all blooming night," the guard grunted as he threw a towel. "Follow me."

Jason wrapped the towel around his waist and followed the guard. He felt nervous. The shouts were getting louder, the smells stronger, and the corridors seemed colder.

What a difference a day makes. He smiled to himself.

Only yesterday he had passed his pilot's license. At eleven he was the youngest person in Britain ever to achieve this. Unlike a driver's license, there was no age minimum on a pilot's license. The flying lessons had been a gift from his father. They had been easy for Jason after he had spent so many hours in flight simulators. The technical side he found hard but he had never expected it to be easy.

But that was yesterday. Today he was working undercover for SYUI. His father, Lieutenant Raymond Steed, was away on the navy aircraft carrier HMS *Ark Royal* and knew nothing of this. His last word was that Jason should have nothing to do with SYUI as he was too young and had already done enough for his country. However, Young's insistence and Jason's eagerness to work for SYUI had got the better of him.

SYUI had heard about an extremely large shipment of cocaine

coming into Britain. The tip-off had led them to believe that Lin Cho, the Triad leader in London, had masterminded the whole dirty operation. The Triads in Britain were part of the Wo Shing Wo organization. They owned bars and illegal gambling halls, sold drugs, and ran a protection racket. They supposedly offered shop owners protection from robberies. In practice, however, they charged a fortune. If a shop owner refused to pay, his shop would get robbed and the store owner beaten or worse. Lin Cho's son, Andrew Cho, was serving time in juvie. It was Jason's job to get close to Andrew and find out where and when the large shipment was coming.

They arrived at a storeroom, a large, high-ceilinged room with whitewashed walls and a cement floor. Jason was given three pairs of socks, underwear, three gray T-shirts. The T-shirts had originally been white but after having been washed over and over with gray socks and overalls, they too had turned gray. He was also given gray shapeless overalls. He got dressed and rolled up his pant bottoms because they were much too long. His pair of black tennis shoes, fortunately, fit.

"Right, lad, off to see the governor, come on, it's late and he'll be wanting to go home."

"Maybe I can go home too, sir," Jason said forcing a smile.

"You are too small to be cocky, lad. If you want to survive in here, you will do yourself a favor and keep your trap shut," he shouted.

"Yes, sir," he replied quietly with his head bowed.

He rolled up his sleeves so that his hands were free and followed the guard down another hallway. They stopped outside a large oak door with a brass plate with the words: Governor Brown. The guard knocked and waited until he heard a "come in."

"This is another new one," The guard said, walking in and reading from a brown file in his hands. "Let me introduce Mr. Jason Steed, sir. Repeat shoplifter, sir. Four weeks."

Jason actually felt guilty even though he was innocent. If Young was right, then the governor was the only man inside the juvie who knew Jason was working undercover.

"Okay, Johnson, leave us for a while. I want to tell him how I want him to behave and explain the rules," Brown replied. "Sit down, Steed, take a cookie." He gestured for Jason to sit down and took the lid off a metal tin full of chocolate-chip cookies.

Then the governor began to laugh. His pale, strangely featureless face turned red and he pushed his fingers through his gray curly hair. Jason, not sure what the problem was, took a cookie.

"Sorry there must be a mistake," the governor said. "I was told that a Jason Steed was coming here and working for SYUI."

"That's right, sir," Jason said with a mouthful of cookie.

"But you're…You're what? Eleven? Twelve? What can a little blond-haired, blue-eyed boy like you possibly do? How can you look after yourself? No, It's out of the question. I can't put you in a cell with Andrew Cho. You'll be dead by morning. We have an arrangement. He keeps out of trouble and doesn't hurt the other inmates, and in return he has a cell to himself. He will kick you from here to kingdom come." He laughed again, which annoyed Jason.

"Do you really think SYUI would put me in here if I couldn't look after myself?" Jason said. "I'm a black belt in judo, jujitsu, and shotokan, and I hold a third dan black belt in tae kwon do. SYUI went to a lot of trouble to get me to go along with this. I would much rather be in my own home with a housekeeper and indoor pool. Plus I attend one of the best schools in the country. *This* is by no means a vacation for me."

Brown examined Jason. He was clearly impressed.

"If you're sure you can take care of yourself. Well, huh…No one will suspect you, that's for sure." He snorted. "But…no special treatments. Once you leave my office, you are on your own. I will treat you like everyone else. If you get hurt, don't come crying to me." Brown spat out his words and sprayed over the cookies. Jason made a mental note not to eat anymore.

"I know…I have a job to do, sir."

He was taken to the cell blocks. The other inmates were playing cards or table tennis or arm wrestling. He followed the guard up a metal stairway carrying his bedding. A few boys watched him as he walked past.

"Here we are, home sweet home. Although I have no idea why the gov has put you in with Andrew Cho. He's not going to like it one bit. Good luck," the guard said and ushered Jason into the cell.

Jason looked around. The top bunk was made up; the bottom bunk had just a thin stained mattress with underwear and socks placed out neatly. The cell had a toilet in the corner and a small stainless steel sink. A single toothbrush was lying on top of the sink. Jason removed the clothing from the thin mattress and placed it on the top bunk and made up his bed. He had only been in for a short while and already he hated it.

"What the—" Cursed a spotty-faced, red-haired boy in the

doorway. It was Russell Watson, a sixteen-year-old boy. This was Russell's second time at juvie; he was sentenced to three months like Andrew Cho, although Russell had been sentenced for stealing cars. Andrew had been sentenced for assaulting a police officer after being caught kicking a store owner half to death.

"Hello," Jason said not making eye contact.

"You can't touch Cho's stuff. What on earth are you doing in there?" Russell cursed.

"Home sweet home." Jason grinned.

"Are you trying to be funny, shrimp?" he cursed again.

"No."

"You're dead, shrimp. He will kick your 'ed in. He has a cell to himself."

Jason ignored the remark although he was getting concerned. The cell was very small. If Andrew started a fight, he was unsure if he had the room to fight back. Russell walked off talking to himself. Jason lay back on his bunk. He was tired. He hadn't slept much the night before due to worrying about being held in juvie. The day before had been such a great day, seeing Catherine in the morning and then passing his pilot's license in the afternoon. He closed his eyes for what seemed like minutes but was probably half an hour when he was woken by voices in his cell.

"See I told you. You got a little shrimp in your cell and he's moved yer clothes," Russell said loudly. Jason opened his eyes and sat up.

"You need to thank god you are so small" Andrew Cho shouted at Jason. "Get your things and get out of my cell. I will be back in five minutes and you had better just be a bad memory."

Andrew was Chinese but spoke with an English accent. He had short dark hair and chocolate brown eyes and acne on his face. Jason thought he was tall for a fifteen year old. Andrew and Russell walked off. Jason said nothing.

I guess I had better get to work and show them I can't be messed with. He followed them down the metal stairway to a large open hall, trying to think of a way to start a fight.

Many of the boys were chatting and laughing in groups. They all wore the same black tennis shoes and gray overalls. Some sat around tables, playing cards. A few played table tennis while others watched. Jason noticed Andrew and Russell with a group of similar aged boys. They all wore their collars up and sleeves rolled up. Russell was bullying a smaller boy. He twisted the boy's nipples through his clothing. In obvious pain, the boy pleaded for mercy. He was made to call Russell all sorts of grand names before Russell finally let him go after a final twist. The boy fell to the ground amid laughs, wiping the tears from his cheeks.

Jason stared at Russell. He never liked bullies, and this was enough to give him the excuse he needed. After a few minutes, Russell noticed and looked at Jason, then looked away. Jason kept the stare. After a moment, Russell noticed that he was still being glared at.

"What's 'e looking at? Hey, shrimp. What you looking at?" Russell shouted to Jason. Jason shook his head from side to side and gave a dirty disgusted look.

"He's asking for it," Russell said and started to stride toward Jason. Andrew and the other boys in the group watched.

"So what you looking at, shrimp?" he sternly asked again.

"Sorry I was staring, but I guess you must get that a lot, being that you're so ugly. Did they throw out the baby and keep the afterbirth when you were born?" Jason asked smiling broadly and slowly raising himself on his toes.

Russell's face went bright red, his eyes popping out of his skinny face. He cursed at Jason and threw a punch. Jason ducked and spun around on his left leg and carried out a full roundhouse kick and made contact under Russell's chin. Russell's head jerked back, his teeth clacked together, and he fell on his back. He must have bitten his tongue, because blood started to pour from his mouth. Russell was quick to get to his feet and ran at Jason swinging wildly with his fists. Jason stood firm and blocked each blow with his arms. He then counterpunched Russell, catching him square on the nose.

Again Russell cursed at Jason. With blood running from his nose, he picked up a chair and swung it in Jason's direction. Jason ducked again, dove to the floor on his hands, and spun his legs around, sweeping Russell's feet away from him. Russell's legs were thrown up into the air. He fell heavily onto his back. Jason pounced on his prey, landing with his knee in Russell's chest. He threw four incredibly fast punches to Russell's face and climbed off him.

"Hmm, some improvement to your face now," Jason joked. A roar of laughter went up from the other boys who started to gather around them. They went quiet and moved back when, Andrew slowly approached.

"Shrimp, pretty good. What form of karate do you practice?" He asked with arms folded.

"The name is Steed, Jason Steed. If we're to be roommates, *you* need to know that. I practice tae kwon do".

Cho nodded and studied Jason while deep in thought. He ruled the juvie; no one had dared speak to him like this before. He watched Jason walk back up the metal stairway and then focused his attention on Russell.

"You are pathetic." Andrew shouted at Russell, who was trying to get up from the floor with one hand, the other hand holding his bloody nose. "You let a little kid like that do that to you. You're an embarrassment. I can't be seen going around with you. Find yourself some new friends,"

Andrew waited until it was bedtime before returning to his cell. "You're still here then, shrimp?" he said from the doorway of the cell. "I thought I told you to get out. Just because you kick the stuffing out of Watson, you think you can ignore me?"

Jason ignored him. He sat on the bottom bunk picking the blisters on his feet. Andrew slowly entered and stood in a fighting stance, glaring at Jason.

"I told you my name, Andrew; it's Jason, not shrimp. You're Chinese—do you want me to call you Take Away?

Andrew glared and raised his top lip. He was about to attack Jason when the cell door slammed and Jason heard two bolts being drawn across. "Night lads, pleasant dreams," said the prison guard. "Good luck, blondie," Jason could hear the guard's footsteps fade into the distance. Suddenly everything was silent. He was alone with Andrew.

Andrew looked at Jason. He was bemused by him—this little pretty boy did not seem to have a care in the world and was not threatened by him.

"I don't get it. You not only move into my cell, kick the stuffing out of Watson, you now call me Take Away? Do you have a death wish? Have you any idea who I am?"

Jason stood up. He looked up at Andrew and forced a smile. "I've no idea why they put me in with an older boy or who you are and I don't really care. Don't blame me for being put into your stinking cell. I am not a shrimp. I'm just younger than you. We can either fight it out or we just make the most of it. I would rather be in with someone my own age as well, but what can I do about it?" Jason held out his hand.

Andrew ignored it and walked over to use the toilet cursing under his breath. He didn't speak as they both got undressed and climbed into their bunks.

Jason was shaking. He was still nervous. Young had told him that Andrew and his father where ruthless. If Andrew wanted to strangle him in the night, he was big enough, and Jason would have a tough job fighting him off. It was another three hours before he finally got to sleep.

During the next few days, Andrew said nothing to Jason. He ignored him and complained to the governor about having to share a cell. The governor explained that there was a of shortage of space and so he had chosen Jason as Andrew's cell mate because he was small and quiet and would not get in Andrew's way. Andrew, although unhappy, had to agree and swallowed the story.

=

George Young held a meeting at the offices of SYUI. He had invited MI5, MI6, and Metropolitan Police Commissioner John

Lock. His direct superior, Simon Caldwell, was also there. Caldwell was Young's age and slim with short gray hair. He was as usual wearing an expensive-looking Italian suit and gold watch. They sat around the large office in the dark looking at images projected on a large screen. Young's voice clipped with authority. His London East End accent dropped slang words at every sentence—something that amused the onlookers. He pointed at a large screen with an unlit cigarette.

"This is Lin Cho, an evil sod and head of the London Triads. He's ruthless and has a reputation for the most violent crimes. Many people inside his organization fear him." He flicked the switch to show another image. It displayed a very large Asian man resembling a sumo wrestler dressed in a suit. He had cropped black hair and his head was thick and his neck seemed to be part of his wide shoulders. "This is Kotang, Lin Cho's body guard and driver. He can crush a feller in his bare arms. I wouldn't want to meet up with this bloke on a dark night."

Next, Young showed an image of a Chinese woman in a blond wig. She was wearing knee-length black leather boots, tight leopard-print pants, and a black leather jacket. "This is Boudicca—she's the head of the entire Triad organization in the United Kingdom. In my view, the most dangerous person in the world. However it's Lin Cho who is organizing the shipment of drugs. We think Boudicca is the same woman who fled China just over five years ago after the tainted milk scandal. She has changed her appearance and her name from Rani to Boudicca."

"Surly this Rani would be keeping a low profile?" John Lock questioned.

"Any normal crook would do that. Any normal crook would have a first and second name. Boudicca is different. She thinks she's above the law. But the new Chinese police commissioner Lin Tse-Hsu is tracking her down and trying to stop her from gaining power back in China. She's been sending huge amounts of money back to China. And I mean huge amounts—in the millions."

"Do we know where the shipment of drugs is coming from and when it will be here?" Caldwell asked.

"It's coming from China," Young replied. "We'll soon know where and when it's being delivered."

He showed another image. It was of a young Asian teenager. "This is Andrew Cho, Lin Cho's only son and a right little terror. He's currently serving time in juvie. We have a man on the inside sharing his cell and befriending him. He'll get the information out of Cho."

"So this inside man, he must be the same age—what sixteen? Seventeen?" Lock asked with his eyebrows raised.

"He's not quite that age, but he's the best. He'll never be suspected. He holds the Victoria Cross and Queens Commendation for Bravery, he's a black belt in more karate disciplines that I can name, and he's the youngest qualified pilot in Britain. He's also fluent in a variety of languages. He's had no weapon training, but on his last mission he seemed to just 'wing it.'"

"Good god, man. You mean that *boy*, what's his name…Jason Steed? He's barley twelve and just got out of hospital!" John snorted. "And he wasn't on a last mission—he just happened to be in the right place at the right time."

"He's the best there is, sir," Young replied turning off the projector. "Plus—let's face it—no one'll suspect him. He'll get the information we need—I stake my reputation on it."

"I hope you're right, Young. We have a lot riding on this." Caldwell sighed.

Young was confident in Jason. He could think of no one else he would trust to go undercover and survive.

About the Author

Mark A. Cooper was born in London and moved with his wife and son to the United States in 2003. When his twelve-year-old son's grades improved after he read the Harry Potter series, Mark decided to encourage literacy with his own novel. He self-published *Fledgling: Jason Steed*, and the novel has enjoyed huge success and a devoted following on the Internet.